The Fox and the Rebound

MARY FRAME

Preface

Dear Reader,

This book contains references to the deaths of a parent and a young sibling as the result illness or accident. There are also references to past toxic and abusive relationships for both main characters and a side character who struggles with former alcohol abuse and addiction.

Thematically, this entire series is a little more heart-wrenching than my other books, but there still is humor—because life is messy, but it's also funny.

I provide this warning so you can make an informed decision about whether to proceed. If you would rather read something more lighthearted, please check out the Imperfect Series or The Dorky Series if you haven't already!

Take care of yourself,

<3
Mary

CHAPTER
One

The intercom on the corner of the desk beeps. "Mr. Nichols, Miss Fox wishes to speak with you."

I lift my bored gaze from the steady stream of numbers flowing across the screen and frown. "I already spoke with Finley this morning. What does she want now?"

The last conversation we had was pointless. Finley updated me on how the cabins for the camp instructors were nearly complete, contracts for the rest of the renovations confirmed, interviews in progress, and the student quarters were on track to be finished by the end of summer—all of which I knew and I didn't care about anyway. The worst part of the interaction was when Archer, my childhood acquaintance and business associate who now lives with Finley, thrust his way into the conversation between me and Finley to "see how things are going." *Things* being code for my emotional well-being.

"Fine," I said, the best answer I could muster.

He then proceeded to update me ad nauseam on the status of all his personal and professional accomplishments of late. By all appearances, and by his own declarations, Archer is happy living in a run-down house in the middle of nowhere with Finley Fox and her chaotic family. A fact I find both annoying and mystifying.

"It's not Finley," Carson says. "It's Piper. Can I send her in?"

My surroundings brighten subtly, the world coming into sharp focus.

This morning started like every other Tuesday. I got out of bed at five. Drank a high-protein smoothie before running on the treadmill for an hour. Showered. Went down to the third floor to work by precisely seven a.m. Ate avocado toast and egg whites prepared by my chef at nine a.m. It was all typical. Normal. Expected. Ordinary. Gray. Boring.

My whole life has become a series of incremental steps and chores that don't have any meaning and do nothing to hold my attention, yet at just the mention of Piper Fox's name, suddenly I'm off the hamster wheel, where I've been running in a dark room, going nowhere, and am thrust out into the sunshine with the breeze and the trees and limitless possibilities.

Foolish. Ridiculous. Irrational.

Why is she here? We had a tacit understanding to avoid each other after the last time.

I shove the thought away. I can't think of that now, not when I'm about to be confronted with her presence for the first time in three months and eleven days.

"Should I tell her you're busy?" Carson asks.

Piper is out there, listening to the entire conversation, so I resist the urge to snap at Carson. To anyone else, he would sound professional and uninterested, but he's teasing me. I appreciate that he doesn't grovel or behave obsequiously, and I enjoy his brash honesty, annoying as it may be. It's one of the reasons I stole him from his last employer and paid him extensively for the defection.

"Send her in." I glance around my office.

This won't do at all. The room is cold, sparse. No personal photos, all business. The desk is devoid of paperwork and has only a laptop. The whole setup—the stark colors, the size, the raised podium where my desk is, the way my chair is slightly elevated—is arranged to put me in a position of power, not in an obvious way but just enough that the guest subconsciously knows I'm the one in charge.

But using these kinds of nonverbal cues on Piper rubs me the wrong way. It doesn't give me the pleasure it would with anyone else. Quickly, I move out from behind the massive black desk to the sitting area closer to the door. I reposition a file from the table to the chair, and just in time, I sit on the couch, leaving the spot next to me as the only reasonable seat left.

Piper enters, the door shutting behind her. I take a moment to drink her in, keeping my face impassive. I've been a fan of her artwork for many years, and my admiration has leaked into our acquaintanceship. She is petite with delicate sprite-like features. Dark hair frames her oval face, and her eyes are large and expressive. On the surface, she isn't out of the ordinary, but her work has absorbed my interest since the very beginning. She sees things in a way that that tugs at all the emotions I've managed to eliminate to get to where I am today.

I want her in a way that I can't define. It's a pointless, impractical, annoying desire. I built her up in my mind before we even met, when I had seen her art. That must be the reason for these feelings: artistic respect, nothing more.

"Mr. Nichols. Thank you for seeing me. I'm sorry to drop in unexpectedly like this."

Mr. Nichols? She spent almost an entire night wrapped in my arms, and she calls me Mr. Nichols?

"You cut your hair," I say.

She fingers the dark strands, which now fall slightly below her shoulders. "I've wanted to for a while, but I couldn't before because..." She falters, forcing a smile that doesn't quite reach her eyes. "Well, I just couldn't." She glances away.

My mind takes her words and body language apart and turns them over, examining their deeper meaning. Ben, her controlling ex-boyfriend, likely has something to do with her new hair preference and why she didn't change it when she wanted to.

"Please. Have a seat." I gesture to the couch next to me.

She walks over and perches on the edge of the seat, a white-knuckled grip on the strap of her purse.

My gaze sharpens on the delicate shadows under her eyes. "You haven't been sleeping well."

The corner of her mouth twitches. "Have you?"

I've never slept well, a fact I inexplicably shared with Piper Fox three months and eleven days ago, in the dark of night, under the watchful glow of an ancient lamp in the Fox living room. I have been trying to erase that night from my mind, mostly by avoiding the woman sitting next to me.

I incline my head. "Touché."

She shifts on the seat. "Have you heard anything from —" She clears her throat. "Have they shipped any of my pieces yet?"

"I received confirmation that the scheduled pickup is Monday. They should arrive at the gallery by next week— Thursday, most likely."

Her shoulders relax a notch. "You don't think he'll try anything else—delay further?"

"He can try all he likes. No one breaks a contract with me without severe consequences." The words emerge like the slice of a knife, fast and clipped.

She blinks, flinching.

For the best, I tell myself even as an uncomfortable thorn twists in my stomach.

She doesn't need to say his name for me to know who she's asking about. Ben—the aforementioned ex-boyfriend who is also her ex-manager. The man is the epitome of a weak-minded, idiotic tool.

"Has he been bothering you?"

"No." She opens her mouth, pauses for a second, then shuts it.

"But?"

One slim shoulder lifts. "At first, he called me every day, multiple times a day. I blocked him. Then he would use random phones. I changed my number, and he spammed all my social media and emails. Then it stopped all of a sudden. Until last week."

My jaw tightens. "What happened last week?"

"He sent a package."

"To Mindy's?" Last I knew, Piper intended to stay with her sister in the city.

She nods. "The texts have started again, from a number I don't recognize. They're generic—just *hi, how are you* kind of things—but I know it's him." Her shoulders droop. "I don't know how he found me or my number. I changed it."

A whisper of unease slithers through me. "What did he send you?"

Pink tints her cheeks. "Jewelry and clothing, a note about how he still loves me and he's changed and wants to make it up to me. I sent it back. He'll give up eventually if I keep ignoring him. It's probably nothing to worry about. I tend to overreact lately, and Ben knows how to get under my skin."

The more she speaks, the more my spine stiffens. "You are not overreacting. You should always listen to your instincts." Concern loosens my tongue. "Mindy's apartment—is there a doorman? Some kind of security?"

"No."

I frown. "You could stay here."

"No." The refusal is immediate. "I can't do that."

I switch tactics. "I can hire a bodyguard. Someone could be with you at all times."

She grimaces. "Oh, no. That's not necessary. It's fine. Ben's all the way across the country. Besides, I rarely leave the apartment without Mindy. Please don't worry about it. I shouldn't have mentioned it."

The urge to press the issue shoves at me, but I swallow my arguments and counterpoints. "Is that why you came here?"

Her visit doesn't quite track. She could have called or gotten this information from Carson. *Why stop by unexpectedly only for this after months of silence?*

She bites her lip, and I home in on her mouth. Her lips are perfect, pink, and heart shaped.

"Um. Well, partly. There is one other thing I needed to… ask." She swallows.

I track the motion, noting the fluttering pulse in her neck, the hitch in her breath.

She inhales and then meets my gaze, her spine straightening, her chin lifting. "I want you."

My heart, the fractured organ long silent, thumps in my chest.

CHAPTER

Two

Oliver

Three Months and Eleven Days Earlier

I can't sleep. Slumber is an eternally elusive state even when I'm at home, resting on a custom-designed mattress and two-thousand-dollar D. Porthault sheets. But trying to sleep on a cramped, lumpy, ancient child-sized couch with the scent of ten thousand family dinners oozing like invisible fog from its depths? Impossible.

What could have compelled me to agree when Finley offered me this pitiable excuse for a resting place? Mindy Fox left for the city earlier in the day. I should have followed her lead and returned to my building posthaste.

This five-bedroom house should have been big

enough for all of last night's guests, but two of the rooms are never used, left as shrines to their former occupants. That leaves three bedrooms, one for Archer and Finley, one for Piper, and the last for Mason, who was dragged here all the way from LA to celebrate Easter with the Fox tribe.

Taylor, yet another Fox sister, is sleeping in her van out front. It's a full house. A full, chaotic, noisy house.

Yet... if I'm being honest with myself, I chose to stay the night here, forgoing all my usual comforts, because I didn't want to leave. Watching all of them interact is like visiting a zoo full of exotic creatures, their behaviors bizarre, unfamiliar, and mysterious, and intriguing.

The floorboards groan, and I crack my eyes open a slice. A figure, ashy in the darkness, separates from the stairs. My ears strain for the soft tread of footsteps marking their way through the living room en route to the kitchen.

It's obvious who my fellow insomniac is, based on the size of the frame and the way she moves through the space, dim as it is. Piper.

I should ignore her. Feign slumber. She'll go back upstairs, and I'll continue to lie here in the darkness, alone.

"Can't sleep?" The words are propelled out of me without my conscious will.

She halts halfway between the stairs and the kitchen, only a handful of steps away from where I'm lying on the couch. One hand goes to her chest, and she releases a shaky chuckle. "No. Hardly ever. You?"

"Same." I sit up, self-conscious in a plain white T-shirt,

my sleep pants covered by an old ratty quilt. "Sorry to startle you."

"It's fine." She pauses. "I was going to make some tea." She stands there, staring at me, making no move to actually commit to the task.

"Okay," I say since it seems she requires some sort of response.

"Did you want some?"

Say no. "Yes."

She flicks on an old lamp near the wall between the living room and kitchen, and it casts a buttery glow over her wan face, illuminating the oversized gray sweater that hangs on her small frame and the soft pink leggings that cling to her form.

I shift to stand, but she stops me with a lifted palm. "Stay. It won't take long for the kettle to heat. It's more comfortable in here. Chamomile okay?"

I nod.

Comfortable isn't the most appropriate adjective, but she's not wrong. The kitchen has no seating, and the dining table on the other side of the living area is covered in detritus from egg coloring and dinner. The lumpy couch and faded recliner are, in fact, the best options.

Within minutes, she's back with a mug in each hand, passing one to me. I expect her to sit in the recliner to the side of the sofa, but instead, she sinks into the couch next to me.

"Thank you," I murmur.

"You're welcome." She blows on her tea.

I hold my cup in both hands, making a valiant attempt to keep my eyes forward, nerves singing in my veins. I'm never nervous. Somehow, this fragile creature is responsible for crafting the most gut-wrenching sculptures I've ever seen. It boggles the mind. She's like a puzzle I can't quite solve. The pieces don't match, yet I know they fit together.

"Do you have a hard time sleeping in strange places?" she asks.

"I have a hard time sleeping anywhere."

She turns. "Why?" Her voice is low and intimate.

I concentrate on the warm cup cradled in my palms. She doesn't press me to answer. Something about Piper hammers at my self-restraint. All the emotions I've kept under tight control transform into a beast that wants to come out of hiding and bask in her sunshine. I'm both captivated and alarmed. I have no room for *feelings*. They are decidedly bothersome.

"He used to wake me up randomly."

Every cell in my body startles to awareness.

"Early on in our relationship, before we moved in together, he would call me in the middle of the night." Her gaze moves to the wall where the blank TV hangs. "It was always under the guise of being thoughtful. He would say he wanted to talk because we were both so busy, and he wanted to spend time with me. He missed me." One side of her mouth tips down. "I thought it was sweet." She stops, considers. "No. He convinced me it was sweet and normal. But then if I put my phone on silent because I had an early meeting or plans the next day, he would accuse me of not making him a priority, of not caring, of cheating, even. My need for sleep—any excuse or obligation—didn't matter because he made me believe I was the one being cruel to him."

She sips her tea, and I trace the simple movement, roaming over her jawline, her neck, her long, delicate fingers cupping the mug. Her head turns in my direction, her neck resting back against the couch.

"I wish I could punch him again."

She faces me and smiles, the simple movement lighting her from within. Her bottom tooth is slightly crooked, the imperfection making her more real and somehow pure. I'm knocked senseless for a few seconds.

"I wish you could, too, and that I could join you." She sighs. "Lord knows kicking him in the balls would be cheaper and more satisfying than therapy."

Her dry tone is so surprising I almost laugh. *How long has it been since I laughed?*

She continues. "I can't figure out how I fell for it, for him. How could I have let him turn me into such a passive creature who second-guessed every move and thought?"

"It never starts badly. Controlling people begin by love bombing and then use their good deeds like sunshine to make the seeds of manipulation grow."

Her eyes widen. "How do you know?"

The dry words fall out before I can stop them. "I have experience with all the toxicity humanity has to offer."

I shouldn't have said it. I search for the pity in her expression, and finding none, I relax, relief curling through me when she doesn't fawn or try to get more information about me. It's the only explanation for why I finally answer her first question.

"I can't fall asleep because I've had to be constantly on alert for threats in my immediate environment." When you're asleep, you're vulnerable to those who might hurt you.

She sets her cup on the coffee table. "I don't have any issues falling asleep, but I can't stay asleep for long. Then once I wake up, it's all over."

"My problem is the opposite. I can't fall asleep, but when I do, I'm out like a light."

She shifts closer, the corner of her mouth tipping up. "I bet I can help you fall asleep."

My brows lift at the suggestion, my body heating almost instantly. "Can you?" My voice is low, intimate.

"I didn't mean it that way. Now my mind is in the gutter, and I can't get it out." Her cheeks flush, and she leans into me, nudging me with a soft elbow.

My brief romantic interludes have been few and far between—too far between. Just her elbow against my arm is inciting a reaction.

"Then what are you suggesting?" I ask.

She takes the untouched tea from my hands and places it next to hers on the table.

"Lie down and put your head in my lap." She shifts on the sofa to give me room.

I stare at her. *She wants my head in her lap?* I'm already half-hard from her statement that she can help me sleep, not to mention her proximity and casual touches, mild as they are. If we get any closer, I might melt into a puddle at her feet.

To her, this is just an interaction shared between friendly acquaintances. This is what Piper and her family do—they laugh, tease, and touch with affection. I can't remember the last time I've been hugged or touched in any way other than shaking hands for business reasons.

She pats her lap. "Come on, Oliver. Trust me."

Trust me. Loaded words. I don't trust anyone. Not really.

I should resist—snap at her, scare her away. But the way she watches me is sweet and trusting, even hopeful. Her affection is like a drug.

It's only because I haven't been with anyone in a while and crave any touch, not just hers. At least, that's what I tell myself, allowing myself to give in because it means nothing. I turn around and angle back carefully, resting my head on her upper thighs and focusing all my attention on the ceiling.

She smiles down at me. "Close your eyes."

After a few seconds, I comply.

She smacks my shoulder lightly. "You're so tense. If you get any more rigid, you're going to vibrate onto the floor. Relax."

I press my lips together, trying not to think about things that are *rigid*, and do my best to ease my tight limbs. It must be good enough because a moment later, her fingers thread through my hair, rubbing and massaging my scalp in gentle strokes. Her thumbs press against the center of my forehead, near the eyebrows, applying pressure before smoothing down and out toward my temples, where they circle for a few long, blessed minutes.

I nearly groan. *What is this sorcery?* I've never felt anything like it. I almost forget how turned on I am.

Once my head relaxes, the rest of my body follows, loosening into jelly, the tension flowing out like water through a sieve. Time ceases to have meaning. Between the press of her fingers, the heat of her body, and the calming scent of tea, I can finally fall asleep.

CHAPTER
Three

Piper

The Next Morning

My neck hurts. Something lumpy and uncomfortable is digging into my side. I can't move my legs. They're being weighed down by a heavy, heated object.

I blink my eyes open, and there's nothing but white. *Holy hell—I've gone blind.*

I blink. *No, wait.* It's a T-shirt. A white T-shirt. It's moving rhythmically up and down.

Oliver.

My neck hurts because it's propped up on his bicep. The lump digging into my side is the couch. The heavy thing weighing me down is Oliver's leg slung over mine. We're facing each other. I'm on the inside, my back to the sofa, and we're wrapped around each other like longtime lovers.

I'm snuggling with Oliver. Oliver, the billionaire. Oliver, the man who used his private jet to fly across the country and rescue me from my psychotic ex-boyfriend. Oliver, the most fascinating and intriguing person I've ever met, who punched Ben in the face for making a derogatory remark about me. The same Oliver who then let me clean his bloody knuckles and assured me in a low voice that he would never let Ben hurt me again—in a tone that allowed no doubt—all right before he manipulated me and my whole family into going into business with him.

Oliver was dead set on acquiring our family property. He purchased all the parcels around Fox Cottages, and when Finley resisted his offers, he sent in his lackeys to try to convince her to sell. But she wouldn't, despite the fact that she'd fallen behind on property taxes and the whole place was practically crumbling down around her. She couldn't let it go. We grew up here. It's all we have left of our father and Aria.

When Oliver's normal tactics wouldn't work, he sent in Archer to try to seal the deal. But Archer and Finley fell in love—and then we found a way to keep the property in our family and retain majority ownership. First, we agreed to turn the property into a camp for at-risk youth, and then, I agreed to create four pieces for Oliver's gallery in SoHo in exchange for an additional one-percent stake in the summer camp.

I get why he wanted the deal so badly. He was hoping to

create something like the type of camp where he met Archer when they were kids. According to Archer, Oliver has no family left. He lost everyone when he was just a child, and the camp was the only place he wasn't miserable. The goal is admirable even if his methods were a bit calculated.

My heart threatens to beat out of my chest with the combination of anxiety and pleasure surging through my system. Surely, it's loud enough to wake him up. Carefully, I shift my head to bring my gaze to his face. He's sleeping.

I take the opportunity to catalogue his features while he's not in motion. I never get the chance to really scrutinize him. Awake, he's a force of energy, like a supernova, powerful and enigmatic. When he enters a room, the air prickles with intensity.

Not now. His features are softened with sleep, young and serene. There's no hint of the domineering and intense presence that surrounds him like a cloak when he's alert.

My sisters think he's callous and unfeeling, but I'm not so sure. Maybe it's the artist in me, searching for beauty in the darkness, wanting to believe after Ben that not all men are monsters. It's the honesty that gets to me the most. Oliver doesn't pretend to be anything he's not. He's not a liar. Ben lied like it was an art form, a requirement for existence, as necessary as water and sunlight.

After meeting his parents, it was easy to understand why he resorted to lying so frequently. He was an only child, his parents both successful, his mother an attorney, his father a real estate mogul. Both of them demanded perfection in all things. It was no wonder he tossed out lies as if they were confetti and every day was New Year's Eve.

Oliver, for all his eccentricities and surliness, doesn't pretend to be someone he isn't or say things to make himself appear superior or in charge. He doesn't need to. Sometimes, I catch him watching the rest of us, his face dark and wary, like an apex predator that's discovered something peculiar and doesn't know whether to attack or run. He tends to sit just far enough away to listen and observe but not quite close enough to truly be a part of the group.

A door opens and closes in the kitchen. Footsteps tread across the linoleum. Taylor. She slept outside in her VW bus, where she lives most of the time.

I shut my eyes. I'll pretend I'm still asleep. Maybe she'll stay in the kitchen. Maybe she won't come into the living room and ruin this moment. Maybe I can lie here and bask in the fact that I actually slept for more than a few hours for the first time since leaving Ben.

Oliver's breath changes. He inhales slowly, and then the arm on my waist tightens.

Unable to bear it any longer, I have to look. His eyes meet mine, heavy lidded and fuzzy with sleep. His mouth tilts into a semblance of a smile.

Shock slaps me in the face. He *never* smiles—even though what he's giving me now couldn't be described as a full smile but is more like a twitch of the lips. My stomach flips over three times and then fills with hot liquid want.

Oliver is always so pressed and polished and suited up. Here in the gray light of early morning, a line bisects his cheek from where it was resting on the sofa, he has a dusting of stubble on his jaw, and his hair is rumpled.

Damn. He might be the sexiest thing I've ever seen. We gaze at each other for an interminable moment. I want to be the one he always gives that little half smile to.

Then his gaze sharpens on me, his eyes widen, and he jerks away, thudding onto the floor.

I sit up. "Are you okay?"

Taylor appears in the doorway from the kitchen. "What was that? Piper?"

He pops to his feet like a shabby billionaire jack-in-the-box.

"Um." Taylor's gaze darts between the two of us, and she puts a hand on her hip, laughter in her voice. "Do you care to explain this unconventional sleeping arrangement?"

"Excuse me." Oliver's voice is smooth and flat, like we're in a board meeting and not in my childhood living room after he woke up in my arms and promptly fell off the couch. He swipes his overnight bag off the coffee table and disappears down the hall toward the guest bathroom.

Taylor's brows hit her hairline. Her eyes are full of mischievous joy when they meet mine. "You've got some explaining to do."

Four

"I want you."

Oh crap. What did I just say?

"I mean, I need you." My welding torch, capable of reaching six thousand degrees, has nothing on the heat of my face right now. "I mean, I didn't mean that."

"Then why don't you explain what you do mean." His voice is frosty, his face an expressionless mask.

Dammit. I did mean it.

I'm an idiot. I don't know why I was thinking I could show up here after months had passed and he would fall all over himself to speak with me. I thought maybe he cared. I thought we had a moment—more than a moment—but maybe I was wrong. Maybe Ben was right when he said I would never find someone else and no one could want me.

How will I know? How can I tell? I search Oliver's face, but his eyes are unreadable.

My heart accelerates, my palms slicking with sweat. *Now what?*

I need another excuse for coming here. I knew this wouldn't work. I knew I would chicken out. I need another plan.

He's staring at me while I have my inner panic attack, his eyes dark and unreadable, his lips flat and dispassionate.

Quick. Say something, anything. "I have problem with…"

My brain, obviously. Men in general. Creating any kind of art to fulfill the terms of the contract I signed with him. Lustful thoughts about Oliver and an old couch. Pick a problem—there are plenty.

My nerves a raw bundle in my throat, I blurt out the first thing I think of that's a partial truth. "I need somewhere to finish the pieces. For the exhibition. There's no room at Mindy's, and I have nowhere to, uh, work."

He frowns. "Don't they rent artist work spaces for this sort of thing?"

He would know about places like that. They do have rentable studios in literally every borough, dang it. Now I need to elaborate.

Oh, what a tangled web we weave.

"That's what I've been doing, but it's not working. The co-op studio spaces, they're too crowded. Too many people and prying eyes, you know. I need a private place." I swallow, and the words keep going, bubbling out of my mouth like they've developed a will of their own—a terrible, awkward will. "I suppose I could go back to Whitby, but I was already struggling there, and, um, with Finley and Archer and now Jake coming home—not to mention all the construction going on—it will be... I'll be in the way. I'm not sure what to do."

The last sentence is the full truth. I have no idea what to do. I'm lost. Floundering in the dark. And running out of time. I asked for six months to create a few sculptures. That time has been cut in half, and I still have nothing.

I can't tell him the full truth of the matter, but maybe I won't have to. I have the slenderest filament of hope that I can use at least one of the pieces being shipped over from LA —although I can barely remember what I was working on before. Those last few weeks with Ben were like a shadowy nightmare. Now I've woken up, but the dregs of the terror have left a gaping hole of numbness, and the will to create has fled along with my sanity.

If I don't want to lose everything, ruin my reputation, and endanger my entire career all because some asshole ripped my confidence to shreds, I need to get work done. I need to get my mojo back. I was hoping to get my mojo back with Oliver in other ways, as per one of Taylor's litany of suggestions, but obviously, that's not happening.

He's silent, focused on something behind me, the gears shifting behind his gaze as his mind calculates the problem. I catch my breath and use the opportunity of his distraction to check him out. I haven't seen him in months.

He's unchanged, still all sharp lines and precise edges, elegantly lean, with dark hair and thick brows. He's like a sleek jungle cat constantly alert for prey—if a jungle cat wore a bespoke suit and never had a hair out of place. He's always perfectly coiffed, a contrast to my inner mess. I want to ruffle him up, make him lose that meticulous control he wields like armor.

"Make a list of anything you require, and get it to Carson today. I'll have something for you by the end of this week."

What were we talking about? Oh right. I need work space, apparently.

My stomach flips. If he gets it done, that means I'll actually have to do the work or tell him the full truth. Panic flares, along with frustration. *If I can't create, then who am I?*

"Um. Okay."

His phone buzzes between us, and I glance down. He picks it up quickly but not before I catch a glimpse. The display shows *Emma*, and the preview of the message is a series of colorful heart emojis.

Something in my chest twists. Of course, he probably gets a dozen different texts like that from a dozen different women every day.

He sets the phone to the side. "Was there anything else you needed?" His tone is still cool, impersonal.

"No, thank you." I force my legs to propel me to my feet and then make my way to the door.

I slip into the reception area, intending to leave it at that. This couldn't have gone worse, even if I had come here intending to humiliate myself, which I sort of did.

What was I thinking?

I thought he would be different. I thought I could be

alluring, mysterious, seductive. I'm an idiot. A lamppost has more seduction skills than I do.

Carson taps away on his computer at the desk parked right outside the door, his posture ramrod straight.

Oliver follows me out. "Did you drive here?"

Surprised, I halt just beyond Carson's desk. No."

I haven't owned a car in two years. Ben convinced me to sell mine when I moved in with him, since we went everywhere together anyway. I didn't realize at the time that it was one more way to control me.

"I took the subway."

Oliver frowns. "Carson, call Brienne."

"I don't want to put anyone out," I say.

Carson speaks, still typing, his fingers not missing a beat. "You're not. I already had Brienne on standby. She'll meet you at the elevator." He nods down the curve in the hallway.

"Right. Thanks. Bye." I escape this oh-so-uncomfortable conversation and round the bend. Out of sight, I stop to catch my breath.

What is it about Oliver Nichols that turns me into a complete chucklehead? "I want you." I can't believe I said that. *Lord, kill me now.* My face heats, and I cover my cheeks with my hands.

I'm still standing there, trying to pull my shit together, when Oliver's voice echoes down the passageway. "Are you finished with the findings for DataBlocks?" The words are brusque and clear as day.

There are no carpets or anything soft to absorb the sounds. Everything is stark white and shiny, making voices crystal clear. I could probably hear Carson and Oliver's conversation all the way at the elevators at the end of the hall without straining.

"Nope. I won't be able to get it to you until tomorrow morning."

My ears prick, surprise fluttering through me at Carson's abrupt negative.

The response from Oliver is so low I almost miss it. "Why the delay?"

"You gave me twenty-seven other priorities. If everything is high priority, then nothing is."

There's a tense pause, and then Oliver sighs. "You know, I only intended for you to complete half that list."

Carson laughs. "Figures. You're a brute."

My brows lift. If someone Ben considered a subordinate had talked to him like that, he would have flipped his lid.

The seconds stretch. Oliver must have gone back into his office, conversation over.

Making my way toward the elevator, Carson startles me into stopping again. "Did you need anything else?"

I glance back in the direction of the voice, half expecting his question to be directed at me, but no one is there.

Oliver speaks. "No. I'll let you get back to work."

"Does this moment of unusual distraction have anything to do with our last guest?" Before Oliver can make any verbal response, Carson tsk-tsks in annoyance. "Don't glare at me like that—she's not my type. Although, if I wasn't gayer than Christmas at Bloomingdales, I might find myself in a similarly wordless state."

I hold my breath. *Are they talking about me?* If he denies it, I don't want to hear it. If he admits it...

Let's face it—that possibility came to a quick death when I told him I want him and he stared at me like I had bubbles blowing out of my ears. Besides, why would he care about me when he has this *Emma* sending him ridiculous love emojis?

"Miss Fox. Are you ready?"

I nearly jump out of my skin. Brienne. She's nearly six feet tall and impossible to miss, yet I didn't see her coming.

Shit. Please, please, please tell me they didn't hear that.

"Sir." Brienne nods to someone behind me.

Double shit.

I push away from the wall. I can't look him in the eye. My gaze dances around his form standing at the edge of the hallway.

"I was just... thinking here for a second." I need to stop talking. I'm only going to make it worse. "Let's go," I tell Brienne.

I follow her to the elevator, and I don't look back.

CHAPTER
Five

The elevator ride down to the garage is silent yet is loud with the resonating echoes of my embarrassment. Brienne remains stoic, standing next to me, her arms loose at her sides. She's a formidable woman. Her uniform of black pants and black button up makes her look like a ninja. A tall, blond, middle-aged ninja.

If only I hadn't told Oliver I wanted him.

If only I hadn't stood there, eavesdropping on his conversation.

If only I could crawl under a rock and live there for the rest of eternity.

We exit the elevator at the garage level, and she opens the back door of a town car idling nearby.

"Thank you for taking me home."

She heads toward the garage exit. The ride is smooth as silk.

"It's my job. I'm glad to do it." Her eyes crinkle in the rearview mirror.

Curiosity pricks at me. While I'm under contract to create at least four pieces for Oliver's new gallery, he's not my boss. I would consider him like anyone else who's commissioned me to make sculptures, not really an employer. He's also sort of a family friend since Archer grew up with him. Archer isn't technically family yet, but I would be surprised if he doesn't propose to Finley by the end of the year. I can't imagine what it would be like to work for Oliver day in and day out.

"How long have you worked for Mr. Nichols?" I ask.

She pulls out of the garage and onto Fifty-Seventh Street. "Eight years. Best job I've ever had."

"You sound like you mean that."

"You sound surprised."

She turns down Seventh, and it takes a full city block of bumper-to-bumper traffic for me to come up with a response. I want her to tell me more about Oliver without being too obvious that I'm digging. "Oliver strikes me as someone who would be an exacting employer."

"He is. He doesn't talk much except to give orders, but he's fair, and he provides more than adequate compensation."

The dollar is king. That makes sense, I suppose.

The car slows down as we make our way through Times Square. I gaze out the window at the lights and the bustle of the city. The vitality of New York is so different from the energy in LA. The beaches and hills of LA are beautiful, but perception is everything. You can't go on a hike without running into a dozen or so influencers and social-media darlings posing for photos. New York is less pretentious. It moves faster. It's more condensed, as if the energy of all the people living so closely together has been bottled up and is ready to burst at any moment.

We crawl down another block before Brienne speaks again. "Last year, my dad had a stroke."

I blink, surprised at the unexpected topic. "I'm so sorry."

"He's fine now, but he spent some time in the hospital, and he had to go through weeks of physical therapy before they would let him go home. He was a fall risk."

"I'm glad he recovered."

Traffic creeps forward at a snail's pace. The subway would have been faster, but at least I don't have to worry about crowded trains or getting lost.

"Oliver paid for all of it. Everything."

My mouth pops open.

She glances at me in the rearview mirror. "He covered all of my dad's medical expenses, continued to pay my salary when I had to leave unexpectedly, and had a nurse check on my dad every day when I came back to work." She shrugs. "I didn't ask—he just did it. Maybe it was high-handed of him, but I couldn't complain. He made a terrible situation manageable. I don't know any other employer who would bother. Don't get me wrong—he has high expectations, but if you do your job, he's loyal, and he takes care of all of us. You know most of his staff live in the building?"

"No. I didn't know that."

"Two floors of the building are for staff apartments. Nice ones. He furnishes them, too, and definitely doesn't charge even a fraction of what a place by Central Park should be."

I knew he owned the building. I knew he lived on the top floor. His offices are on the floor under that. The second and third floor must be the staff accommodations. The first floor is the garage, where a bunch of vehicles are parked, along with a security office. I thought all the cars were his, but some must belong to his staff.

I take this information and slot it into place with everything else I've learned about Oliver Nichols since I met him back in February. He's a paradox. A physical manifestation of a contradiction that somehow makes perfect sense.

A few minutes later, Brienne pulls up to the curb in front of Mindy's apartment building, nestled in the trendy neighborhood of the West Village.

"Thanks for the ride, Brienne. It was nice to chat with you."

She nods and waves.

I jog up the steps to the four-story walk-up while pulling my keys from my purse, glancing around at the front stoop. Ever since I got that package from Ben, I've been wary and nervous, waiting for him to appear around every corner. I climb the stairs to Mindy's apartment on the third floor, walk inside, and collapse on the overstuffed white couch without taking off my shoes or my purse. Then I stare up at the exposed beams on the ceiling and recap the dire situation I find myself in.

I left my emotionally abusive boyfriend and went back to my childhood home at the tender age of twenty-seven.

I promised to create four major pieces as part of an exhibition for an exclusive gallery owned by billionaire Oliver Nichols.

I'm now living in New York with my sister and mooching off family, and I told Oliver Nichols that I want him and then lied through my teeth about needing space to work when the truth is... the truth is space doesn't matter. I haven't been able to create anything in months. I have no creativity, no impulses, nothing, nada, zilch.

This has never happened to me before. The first time my dad handed me a MIG weld, when I was eight, I knew what I wanted to do. Ideas were as abundant as stars in the universe, ever expanding. I never thought I'd have the time to create every idea that poured into my consciousness. Now I can't even come up with a vague concept.

What if I can never create again? What will I do? Who will I be? Metal sculpting is all I've ever known. I'm an imposter.

Despair pushes me down farther into the couch. I can't believe I told Oliver I want him. To his face.

A laugh bubbles out of me. I need to send him a list of all things I need. Oh, he's going to get a list all right. I'm going to ask for every tool and part I can think of and then some.

My phone dings. I tug it out of my purse.

It's a text from an unknown number: *Did you try it on? I wish I could see how beautiful you look in it.*

My stomach flips and churns with dread, blood roaring in my ears. I force myself to take deep breaths, calming my racing heart, a litany of reassurances scrolling through my mind. *It's okay. I'm okay. He's not here. He's in LA. He's three thousand miles away. He can't hurt me. I can't let him win.*

Once my panicked reaction mellows into mild anxiety, I screenshot the image and then block the number. Not that it will help.

The text refers to the outfit he sent me, a slinky dark-blue evening dress. He always bought me expensive clothes—to show me off, he said. Except when we fought, Ben would hold those same gifts over my head, saying I didn't deserve them. He spent so much time and effort on me, and I could never do the same for him. No matter how hard I tried, it was never enough.

My phone rings, startling me from my thoughts.

"So, what happened? Did you accidently cuddle again?" Taylor asks before I can even offer a greeting.

I shake away thoughts of Ben as memories of my meeting with Oliver rush in, and I groan. Taylor is the only one of my siblings with all the information. She knows about my creative struggles and my preoccupation with moving on from Ben, and she knows I wanted to propose a rebound type of fling with Oliver today.

It's not that I don't trust any of my other siblings—it's just that Finley is like a second mother and Mindy is all about work and responsibility and making good decisions. And

Jake, well, he's still in rehab, but he's getting out any day now.

Taylor is the opposite of responsible. She's a free spirit and the closest to me in age. Not to mention she's the one who walked in on Oliver and the whole snuggling episode.

"No cuddling, but I did tell him I wanted him, then I said I needed him, then he stared at me like I was a freak, so I lied and made him think that I actually need some kind of creative space, only to finish our conversation with him promising to fix my fake problem, followed by me getting caught eavesdropping on a conversation with his assistant."

Silence for a full three seconds. Then Taylor laughs so loud that my ear rings, her hilarity immediately followed by a massive clattering. She's dropped her phone.

I sigh, shutting my eyes and waiting for her to come back on the line.

"Wow. That was a lot to take in. How did all this happen?"

I open my eyes, staring at the distressed brick wall behind the bookshelf on the other side of the living room. "I panicked."

"What are you going to do?"

"Good question. I have no idea." I kick off my shoes.

"I guess you'll have to find someone else to bang."

"Taylor!" I chuckle.

"Someone's gotta say it, Piper. We can't let Ben the bastard be your one and only."

I tug at my T-shirt where it's all bunched up. *Oh.* I never took off my purse. It's still strapped around me. I pull the strap over my head and toss it onto the coffee table. "I know."

"You have to get your inspiration back in time to make some pieces for his gallery opening, which is happening in less than three months now."

"I know," I say again, louder this time.

"This calls for drastic measures."

"Taylor. I. Know." I stop. "Wait. What do you mean drastic measures? How drastic?"

"I'm not saying you should meander your way into an orgy or anything, just, you know, if you can't get Oliver to comply, find someone else. Ben damaged your confidence because he's an asshat from hell. You need a little no-strings fun to shake up your chakras."

I don't want anyone else. I'm drawn to Oliver because he treats me like I'm not broken. He's honest and blunt. He doesn't handle me with kid gloves like my family has ever since I left Ben. I'm not sure I could handle him looking at me like I'm damaged—although the blank face I got today wasn't great, either.

It shouldn't matter. He's as unreachable as a star. And why would he want someone broken like me when he has extreme-emoji Emma?

Ugh. Even the voice in my head sounds whiny and pathetic.

"Really, you should tell Oliver the truth. He'll understand. And then maybe he'll let you play with his penis."

I snort out a laugh. "That's the thing—I'm not sure he will." I bite my lip, thinking.

"We won't let Ben win."

"I know." I *can't* let him win. I will get through this.

You have to plunge headfirst into the hurt to get to the heal. I've gone through this process before. After our sister died, I was consumed with grief, pain, guilt—every emotional color of the rainbow. I dove into the feelings and then molded and shaped them into art. It was cathartic. I can do it again.

But for some reason, it's impossible to confront the elephant sitting on my chest. I look at a blank page, a row of old rusty spoons or bolts, car parts—items that used to spark ideas, making my fingers itch and flourish with inspiration— and I feel... nothing.

"What are you going to tell him when you run out of excuses?"

Anxiety is a bubble in my stomach that never pops. "I don't know. The truth is too embarrassing." And maybe illegal.

What will happen if I can't meet our obligation written in the contract? Will Finley lose our family property? I'm too scared to ask.

"You could always come with me to the Summer Solstice. It's one of the best festivals, and it's on the Fox River. It's, like, meant for us. You'll have fun." She drags out the last word in a singsong voice.

Living in a van by the river with Taylor, though I love her, sounds like a recipe for sibling homicide and won't solve my problems. "I wish I could run away, but I have to stay and find a way to satisfy this contract."

Taylor grumbles. "Work isn't everything. Your mental health is more important. You're hanging out with Mindy too much. She's a workaholic."

The door jangles open, Mindy's heels clicking in the entry.

I sit up. "Speaking of, Mindy's home."

Taylor groans. "Lame. That's my cue. Love you much, but byeee."

The line goes dead. A startled laugh bubbles out of me even as I check my phone. Yes, she did in fact hang up on me.

"Hey." Mindy tosses her keys into the dish on the small table between the kitchen and entry area and sets her purse down. "Who was that?"

I toss my phone onto the reclaimed-wood coffee table. "Taylor."

Mindy grimaces with her nostrils flared.

"That's not pretty," I tell her.

She stretches her face even further, her lips pursing and twisting, nose wrinkling, crossing her eyes. I laugh. I don't bother requesting an explanation for the weirdness with Taylor. I've already tried with both sisters, and neither will fess up.

Mindy isn't exactly the boring workaholic with a stick shoved up her ass that Taylor always says she is, and Taylor isn't the lazy freeloader Mindy thinks she is. Someday, maybe they'll get their differences sorted out, but until then, we all have to put up with their animosity that sprang to life out of nowhere. At least they aren't in the same room together very often, having mastered the art of avoidance.

Mindy pads over to the couch, kicks off her heels and plops down in the chair next to me with a big exhalation.

"How was work today, honey?" I ask.

"Exhausting. How about you?"

"Oh yeah, it was great. Right on track." I force a smile.

"That's good," Mindy murmurs.

She doesn't see my fake cheer because her eyes are shut, her head lolling back on the chair.

"I went to see Oliver today."

She lifts her head. "Why?"

"To talk about the upcoming gallery opening."

"I don't understand how he and Archer can be friends. They're so different."

"They grew up together."

She scratches her head. "Yeah, but Archer is like a white knight, and Oliver is like the black death."

I chuckle. "He's hardly plague-like."

She frowns. "I don't trust him. I don't like that Finley is in business with him or that he roped you into it. It was slimy."

I tap the armrest with my fingers. "He's not that bad. He's doing me a favor."

Her brows dip. "Or that's what he wants you to think. I've talked to people who've done business with him. He has no scruples. He's Machiavellian and manipulative. He doesn't care who he hurts to get what he wants."

My conversation with Brienne disproves Mindy's second-hand judgement, but I don't want to argue with her. I'm tired and hungry and still recuperating from my embarrassing afternoon.

"Well, I have to work with him. I also get to decide who I talk to and when," I say.

She sighs. "I know."

I made this clear to Mindy after talking to my therapist. My family is well-meaning but would also like to smother me in bubble wrap and would prefer that I never speak to any man again or leave the house or do anything that might result in so much as a paper cut. But I have to face my fears. I have to learn to trust not only members of the opposite sex but myself too.

"I talked to Finley this morning." She sits up, tucking her legs under her on the chair.

"What did she say?"

"Jacob will be home from rehab next week. If we can't visit soon, she wants us to commit to driving up on the Fourth of July for a barbeque and family fun times with the whole gang." She grimaces.

"Can you go?"

She shrugs. "I'll try."

"You don't sound real committed."

"If Taylor and I are forced into proximity again, one of us might end up committed."

I sigh and give her a pointed look, which she ignores. "How is Jake doing? Did she say?" I ask.

"Not really. She said he's been a little monosyllabic when they talk, and they can only connect once a week for a short period of time, so it's not much to go on."

"Maybe he'll thaw out a little more once he's home."

"Or he'll get worse when he's around everything that reminds him of Aria and he has more access to booze."

"I hope not."

Guilt swirls inside me like a remorseful tornado. I didn't know how much Jake was struggling or that he'd been drinking so much. I had no comprehension of what Finley was going through, living with him for the past decade. I was too wrapped up in my work, my own grief over Aria's death, and then Dad's passing. And then Ben effectively cut me off from everyone who cared about me.

"You want takeout?" I ask.

"Sure."

"I can order it." I reach for my purse.

She waves a hand at me. "You always get it."

"You're letting me live with you. It's the least I can do." *Especially since this quick visit has turned into a three-month extended stay.*

I shouldn't be imposing on my sister anymore, but I have nowhere else to go. I can't go back to Whitby. I love Finley, and I'm truly happy for her and Archer, but their honeymoon period and lovey-dovey eyes didn't help in the face of my epic failure of a relationship. Not to mention the memories of Dad and Aria in every nook and cranny, which made me smile while simultaneously punching me in the gut. I was too emotionally fragile to be there so soon after leaving Ben.

Naively, I thought that I would have a plan by now, a light at the end of the tunnel, but I have nothing. I mean, I have a decent savings—I never let Ben put his name on my accounts, even though he tried to convince me otherwise. But that money would dry up in a flash if I tried to rent a place in the city, especially since the coffers have nothing coming in to replenish the balance and no income on the horizon. Not unless I can unbreak my brain sometime soon.

"You know I love having you here. It's nice to have someone to come home to," Mindy says.

I have no reason to doubt her statement, but guilt eats at me nonetheless. "If I wasn't here, clogging up your spare room, you might have someone else to come home to. Someone who could do more than mope around and order takeout."

She snorts. "I don't need someone else to come home to. You know I'm married to my job." She opens her eyes, her head tilting toward me. "Speaking of my job, I have to go to this record-release shindig on Friday in Brooklyn. You wanna come?"

Now it's my turn to make a gross face. "I'd rather not."

Mindy chucks a white throw pillow at my head. "Come with me."

I laugh and toss it back at her.

She catches it with one hand. "Come on, Piper. It will be fun. We'll dress up, get the label to send a car for us. You deserve to let loose. You've been working so hard lately."

Ha. Yep. So hard.

"I'll think about it. You want Tue Thai?" I ask.

Mindy sighs at my obvious subject change. "This conversation isn't over. But yes."

I'm already pulling up the app on my phone. "You want the usual?"

"Sounds good. I'm going to go get comfortable." She stops at the door to her bedroom. "Get an extra order of crab Rangoon."

"You got it," I call right before she disappears. A minute later, the shower turns on.

I'm too ashamed to tell her the truth of my creative problems. Mindy is so successful and ambitious, and she would never let anything—let alone a man—get in her way. I don't think she's had a serious relationship since college—she's been so focused on her career.

Her distraction makes it easy for me to hide the truth. I make sure to get home later sometimes so she thinks I'm working when really, I'm eating my bodyweight in Van Leeuwen ice cream while I try to draw inspiration by staring at a blank page. Like sucking concrete through a straw.

Maybe I should go to this party. Oliver is not going to happen. I need to turn my focus in another direction. Maybe this is it. Maybe I'll find my muse there.

Oliver

"I want you to be in my wedding."

The sentence is unusual enough to jar me from the list of acquisitions I've been feigning interest in. After Carson announced Guy Chapman's presence, I made him wait outside my office for ten minutes, and then I ignored him when he walked in because it pleases me to annoy him.

I lift my attention from the computer. "Is that a question or a demand?"

Guy sits in the black leather guest chair across from me, not intimidated in the slightest. One corner of his mouth tips up. "It's more of a proposal. Does anyone ever demand anything from you?"

Not really. It would make things a lot more interesting if they did. Well, one person has—Piper, when she said she wanted me. Of course, she didn't mean it. Slip of the tongue. But then she was listening to my conversation with Carson and... I shake the memory away.

This conversation is noteworthy if a bit strange. *A wedding? Me?*

Instead of giving an answer, I stall for time to consider his proposition. "When are the nuptials taking place?"

I need to proceed cautiously. People don't ask me for these types of favors. People don't want to spend time with me—they want my money. This is different, which in and of itself is interesting, at least. But I can't help but wonder if there's an ulterior motive. Although I've known Guy for years. He's not the type to prevaricate, and he has his own money.

"We're thinking this fall, when the trees start to change, somewhere upstate. So what do you say—will you be a groomsman?"

Confusion clouds my thoughts. "Why me?"

"Because we're friends."

We are? I don't voice the question out loud. I don't want to expose my own ignorance. Recent experiences have led me to believe I don't understand the meaning of the word.

Friendship. The technical definition is a state of mutual trust, respect, and affection. All of which I don't feel for anyone, thus negating the whole *mutual* aspect of the word.

I've known Guy since high school, and we've done business together, but that's it. I might consider Archer and Mason something akin to friends, but we're only acquainted because we suffered similar childhoods. I can call on them for favors without question, and they can do the same with me. But we don't spend time together, except for this past Easter, and I doubt that will be repeated. We share a pact of sorts. Nothing more, nothing less.

Guy speaks in the face of my continued silence. "As much it pains me to admit it, you are one of the reasons Scarlett and I are together."

I tap the back of my pen on the edge of the desk. "I discouraged the connection."

Guy grins. "Which basically drove me right into her arms." His grin dips slightly, his eyes steady on mine. "You're the only one, other than me or Scarlett, that could walk Emma down the aisle."

I frown. "You're using your little sister to get me to agree?"

"Is it working?"

I cross my arms.

"Come on, Oliver. She's picky about people in general, but she loves you. Ironic, since the rest of the world thinks you're an ass."

This almost eliminates my frown—not because Guy called me an ass, although that's part of it, but because Emma does like me. Every time I see her, she wants to play with me—as much as she's capable of play. And she texts me almost daily. Though her nerve disorder leaves her unable to speak, and though she struggles to walk or even reach for things, Emma sure knows how to use a cell phone and iPad. We've become pen pals of a sort, communicating through emojis.

I don't make decisions based on emotion. There's no benefit to being Guy's groomsman. It also feels like giving in. Surrendering is weakness. Yet I'm also oddly pleased he would ask. I don't trust that part of me. That same part led to me ending up with my head in Piper's lap.

Guy stands. "I know you aren't going to understand this, but I do consider you a friend. I hope you feel the same way. People need each other for more than business deals and money and what they can get out of it. Human connection is important."

I stare at him.

He stands. "Even you need someone, Oliver."

"I've survived this long without all that nonsense."

"Have you? Is it enough? Does spending all your time running businesses and living in your office make you happy?" He waves a hand. "Aren't you bored?"

Surprise flickers through me, but I maintain my stony facade. I *am* bored. *How does he know?*

The intercom beeps once. "Mr. Nichols, Miss Fox is on the phone."

Every cell in my body jolts to immediate attention. "Which one?"

Carson is being vague on purpose. I'm sure of it.

"Finley."

Guy points at me. "I got it. You owe me one since you stole my assistant." He jerks a thumb in the direction of the door.

"I didn't steal anyone. I offered Carson a better life than the one you peddled to him."

Guy lounges back, resting his ankle on his knee. "I'm not leaving until you at least agree to think about it."

Carson cuts in through the speaker. "Shall I take a message?"

"No. Guy is on his way out." I glare at him.

Guy lifts his brows, waiting for an answer. "Well?"

"Fine," I grind out. "I'll think about it." *And then say no eventually.*

He grins. "I'll call you next week."

"Whatever," I mumble as he exits my office, leaving the door open.

"Put Finley through."

The phone rings, and I put it on speaker. "Two times in one week? To what do I owe the torture?"

She laughs. "Such a charmer. I wanted to talk to you about intersession camps."

"What do you mean?"

"As you know, we've planned for Camp Aria to be mainly a summer camp, but I was thinking during the fall or winter break, we could have shorter camp sessions. Just a week long or so. We could also consider hosting weekend retreats that focus on one skill set, like a two-day cooking camp or a two-day camping-and-hiking retreat."

Working with Finley has been more productive than I anticipated, especially after our somewhat rocky start. When I say *somewhat rocky*, I mean she nearly killed, maimed, or tortured the business associates I sent out in vain attempts to purchase her property early this year. I finally called in a favor from Archer, one of the best negotiators I've ever known, and he ended up moving in with Finley and bargaining for a joint partnership to please us both. I even gave up a controlling percentage in exchange for some of Piper's artwork.

Piper. My mind circles back to our conversation earlier in the week. Piper was lying, and she's terrible at it. Something else is afoot, and I want to know what it is. If it's Ben, if he's been messing with her, I will find a way to rip his entrails out through his anus. Metaphorically speaking, of course.

Finley continues. "This way, we can open and run quick camp sessions before next summer as a way to ease into it and work out any kinks."

"It's a good idea."

"Great. I'll iron out the details and send something to you by the end of the week." She stays on the open line, and I wait for her to end the conversation.

I tap my fingers on the desk. "If that's all—"

"Hang on a sec. Archer wants to talk to you."

"Fine." I recline back in the chair and wait.

There's murmuring and a noise that sound suspiciously like lips meeting before the phone changes hands.

"When are you coming to visit?" Archer asks, forgoing any greeting.

"You mean have an in-person meeting with Finley regarding the ongoing status of our project? I don't see a need."

Archer sighs. "I'm not talking about business. Everything is running smoothly here. Well, as smoothly as any construction project can go. You could come just to hang out."

I frown, baffled. "I don't hang out."

"Maybe you should try it. Stay a few days. You know, it's this thing people do. It's called taking a break."

"Why?"

"Why not?"

Is he an idiot? "Because I have other obligations, for one."

Archer chuckles. "You have assistants for your assistants."

"I do not."

"I'd like one of those, actually," Carson calls out.

Archer continues. "You of all people could use a few days off. Besides, Jake is home now, and we're trying to keep him occupied and distracted."

Jake is the only Fox brother out of all of the siblings. Poor bastard is surrounded by sisters. Unsurprisingly, he's had some personal issues—drinking himself to oblivion, generally being a nuisance—and he was in a car accident back during the winter. He broke his femur and did a stint in rehab. All of which has nothing to do with me.

"This sounds like a you problem," I say.

His voice lowers. "I'm trying to come up with ways he can contribute to the camp, but it's not enough. We need to keep him busy, active, keep his mind off drinking, you know?"

My frown turns into a scowl. It's like he's not even listening to my rude remarks. "And you think I'm the person to ask for advice?"

"I thought you at least might know how to distract someone. Piss them off so they don't think about anything but how to maim you. Or maybe you have people who could come up with ideas on, I don't know, activities?"

I tug at my tie, the normally comforting weight of my suit suddenly restrictive. What's with today? First Guy wants me in his wedding, and now Archer is coming to me for help with his surrogate family. I might as well toss him a bone, if only to get rid of him.

"Carson!" I call. "What's that thing you do on Tuesdays and Thursdays?"

He calls out something, but his voice cuts off at the end, and he starts coughing.

I frown. "Cross-stitch?"

"Huh," Archer says, surprised. "I guess that's worth looking into. Thanks. Listen, think about coming up for a visit, okay? No work, just fun. Talk later." The line goes dead.

Carson appears in the doorway, drinking from a bottle of water. "I said Cross*Fit*. Not cross-*stitch*."

I wave him off. *Whatever.*

He mutters something under his breath before saying, "You got a delivery. One of those edible arrangements, a bunch of fruit shaped like flowers."

"From whom?"

He shrugs. "No card. Delivery guy wasn't one of our regulars."

I frown. "Toss it. Anything else?"

"Also, Arnold called while you were on the phone. He said Ben is here in the city."

"Does he know when he arrived?"

"Flight records show about two weeks ago."

An irritating mixture of emotions roll through me. I'm angry at Ben. I'm worried for Piper. The fear feeds the anger, growing into a flaming beast in my chest. This is why I don't do *feelings*.

"Where is he staying?"

Carson sighs. "At the Walker Hotel in Greenwich."

My jaw clenches. Too close. There is no good reason for Ben to be in New York, staying that close to Mindy's apartment. I don't like it.

"I want Arnold to follow her when she leaves Mindy's. Tell him I need daily updates by five and immediate updates if anything changes."

Carson pauses, watching me. "Are you sure about this?"

"Yes." I glare at him.

We've already had this conversation. I agreed not to overreact and have her tailed unless there was just cause. I have more than just cause in the form of a stalking, narcissistic exboyfriend. Carson insists it's a terrible idea to have her followed without her permission, but I have to keep her safe. It isn't a choice—it's a compulsion. Besides, it's only to keep an eye on her when she's out and about. Arnold is off the clock once Piper is safely in Mindy's apartment and not alone.

Carson lifts his hands defensively. "You're the boss."

I rein in my reactions and focus on the tasks that need to be accomplished. Something I can control. "How is work on the studio space?"

"On schedule. It should be done by tonight."

"Good."

Piper emailed an extensive list of requirements. I wasn't sure even Carson could handle it, but I should have known better. Carson lingers in the doorway.

"Did you need something else?" I don't hide my exasperation.

He sighs. "I guess not."

I shouldn't put up with the insubordination, but he processes twice the amount of work in half the time my last ten assistants needed.

Carson finally disappears from the doorway. The distant sound of typing reaches me as he gets back to work. I open my laptop and pretend to review quarterly numbers, but instead, my mind returns to Piper.

Work is boring. The constant chase for more wealth and new business ventures has lost its appeal. But Piper... she isn't boring.

The rest of the day is a blur of phone calls, meetings, and errant thoughts about Piper. Carson leaves for the night, but I keep working—pretending to work—in a futile attempt to wear myself out. It doesn't work.

Years ago, I got involved in art dealing, and while I made some money, I never really understood it. I had to hire someone to explain to me what was good and bad. People would spend millions on scribbles of paint a cat could have created, while a decent rendition of a sunset or skyline would be called trash. It defied logic.

Then I saw one of Piper's pieces and was truly struck by what art could be—what it could represent and the emotion it could evoke. It was like someone had torn into my very soul, ripped out all my hidden vulnerabilities, and gave them physical form.

And then I met her in person. She wasn't what I'd expected, yet I couldn't stop thinking about her. Piper is a threat to the self-discipline I've honed into a sword. At the same time, she's like the finest jewel that I want to take and hoard.

I look up from my laptop. The windows are flush with darkness, broken only by city lights. These conflicting emotions are precisely why I need to stay away from Piper Fox.

I call security to let them know I'm done for the night, turn off the lights in the office, and take the elevator to the top floor, vowing to not think about Piper Fox for the rest of the evening. Even if I have to pound the treadmill for six hours to run my body into exhaustion, I will wrench my control back.

I exit the elevator and follow the hallway into the open-concept kitchen and living room. Everything is stark and white and blank, almost like a canvas, except for where the interior designer strategically placed plants, expensive artwork, and lighting. I open the oversized stainless-steel fridge and grab one of the prepared nutritionally diverse meals left by my chef.

My phone rings. Arnold.

I answer on the first ring. "Status update."

"I lost eyes on her. She's gone into a private event," Arnold says.

"Is she with anyone?"

"Her sister."

A beat of relief pulses through me.

"There's more," he continues. "I parked and joined the crowd by the red carpet. I saw Ben Simon."

No. The need to protect Piper grips me in a hot fist.

"I won't be able to tell when they leave. They took a black town car exactly like about a hundred other cars at this event. Our best option is for me to watch the apartment for their return."

Usually, he's off the clock once Piper is safely in Mindy's apartment. It's not the most secure location, but the front entrance is decent enough, and Mindy's apartment has multiple locks. Plus, Piper is not alone when she's there.

I don't need Arnold anymore tonight. I can make sure Piper gets home safely. I have to. It isn't even optional at this point.

"Where?" I ask.

"Nowadays, in Brooklyn."

"You're off the clock until tomorrow, then."

"Got it."

We hang up, and I call Brienne. "I need a ride."

Piper

"That's Oliver's ex," Mindy says in my ear, nodding to a stunning woman posing on the red carpet in front of us.

The woman's royal blue dress fits her like a second skin. Her shiny dark hair is a sleek wave down her back. She's tall and glamorous, precisely the kind of woman you'd imagine a billionaire would want on his arm.

We aren't walking the red carpet ourselves, not really—we're creeping in the background and watching while music artists, journalists, and other industry folks pose for pictures and talk to reporters.

"Who is she?" I ask, fiddling with the silvery strap of the dress I borrowed from Mindy and trying not to wince in the matching heels every time I take a step. They fit—Mindy and I are almost the exact same size and have a similar frame—but

I haven't worn shoes this nice in months, and my feet are not happy with the torture.

"Regina Charles. She's the editor of *Rage*."

So, not Emma. Hmm.

Rage is a fairly new fashion magazine that's bold and popular. Regina Charles fits Oliver. Statuesque, magnetic, successful. They would be gorgeous next to each other. Two halves of the same shiny and lucrative coin.

"Who's he with now?" I ask as if wanting to dig the knife a little deeper into my own gut. We skirt a journalist interviewing a pop star and head into the venue.

"No one that I know of," Mindy says.

"Maybe someone named Emma?" I flush.

I shouldn't have asked. I shouldn't care. But I do.

She links her elbow with mine, leaning in to speak into my ear over the rock music blasting an inch beyond what's comfortable. "Not that I know of, but it's hard to say. Regina is the only person that anyone can confirm he's dated, and that's because she blabbed about it all over the place. Oliver is notoriously private. Their relationship didn't last long after that."

We barely make it two steps through the crowd before we're stopped by a twentysomething in a gunmetal-gray blazer paired with a smarmy smile. Basically, a Christian Bale-in-*American Psycho* wannabe.

Mindy introduces us, and I immediately forget his name. They start talking shop. It's all "sync licensing" this and "360 deal" that—music-industry speak that I don't understand and can barely hear over the noise anyway.

I glance around instead. The venue is crowded with an eclectic mix of industry types. Sleek suits and flashy dresses are mixed liberally with jeans and T-shirts. Except of course, they're Dolce & Gabbana jeans and Fendi T-shirts. The way the rich dress down.

Waiters in colorful tuxedos circulate with appetizer trays, and a DJ spins records up in one corner. The center is a giant dancefloor strobing with flashing lights, while more mellow glows perch in the corners. And I locate what must be the bar, all the way on the opposite side, smothered with people.

I've been immersed in glitz and glamour before, back in LA. It's all shiny and nice at first, but there's a hum of false-hood under the glittering veneer. Smoke and mirrors, masks of happiness—it's all for show. None of it feels real.

It's not my thing. It never was. Ben loved parties like this. He liked seeing and being seen. I would much rather be at home, watching a movie, or in the studio creating. If only work were an option right now. If only the blank page wasn't always staring at me, mocking me with its empty space.

Mindy and the suit finish their conversation, and almost immediately, her assistant, Ally, pops in between us. "Thank God you're here. You look amazing, where did you get that dress? We need you. Richard is all coked out and threatening to beat up Justin Timberlake, who isn't here, by the way, but there's some young kid with ramen hair, and Richard thinks he's back in 1998 since he had that whole boy-band thing that fizzled out. We need you to calm him down before he punches some rando in the face. The press will have a field day." She finally takes a breath.

Mindy nods at her then winces at me. "Sorry, Piper. Duty calls. I'll be right back."

I wave her away. "Go on. I'll meet you at the bar."

"I'll be quick."

"Take your time. I'll get us drinks."

Mindy squeezes my hand once before hustling after Ally.

Slipping through the crowd, I head in the direction of the bar. I find a small spot to squeeze myself into between a shaggy-haired cowboy and a handsome couple standing together, the man's arms on either side of the woman, peering over her head to order drinks and then dipping down to kiss her cheek. I turn away.

The last time I was at a swanky party with Ben, I spent too long talking to another metalwork artist, and Ben accused me of flirting with him. "Are you trying to make me look like a fool?" he hissed at me.

Then he froze me out, completely ignoring me the rest of the night while he chatted and schmoozed with everyone else present. It was a common tactic for him—letting me know I did wrong, then pretending everything was fine while the anticipation built until when we would be alone at the end of the night and he could berate and criticize me to his heart's content. Right now, I might be a loser all by myself at the bar, but this is still way better than being with Ben.

The bartender lifts his brows at me, ready for my order. I glance at the shaggy-haired cowboy. He was here first, but he dips his head, gesturing for me to order.

"I'm good," he says, the slightest southern twang shading his words.

"Thanks. Can I get a sparkling water with lime and an old-fashioned?"

The bartender nods, and a few minutes later, I have our drinks in hand, but there's still no sign of Mindy.

"You're Piper Fox," the cowboy says.

Surprised, I turn to face him. "I am." *Please don't ask me what I'm working on.*

The cowboy doesn't quite fit in with the rest of this crowd, and it's not just the hat. His suit is nice enough, if a little worn, like he only has one or two good jackets he brings out for special occasions. His jeans are brand-name but about a size too large, and his boots are dusty. He appears to be around my age, maybe a little older. He's also bright-eyed, eager, and friendly. Something about him reminds me of a puppy. Like a golden retriever. He hasn't been a part of this scene long enough to be dead eyed and discouraged or callous and jaded.

"You look a lot like Mindy," he says.

Mindy and I are similar in more than build. Her nose is a little bigger than mine, her face is less rounded, and her hair is shorter and straighter, but if you put us in a lineup, the similarities would be palpable.

"This is true. Do you work with her?"

"Not yet." The slant of his grin is roguish.

I take a sip of my sparkling water, my brows lifting. "Not yet?"

He rests his elbows on the bar. "Can I tell you something, Piper Fox?"

Curious, I say, "Please."

"I'm not supposed to be here."

I laugh, relaxing a little. "How did you sneak in?" It couldn't have been easy. He would have had to get through multiple security checkpoints not to mention make his way along the red carpet.

"Snuck in with the caterers."

"Ballsy."

He grins at me, which pushes him from merely cute puppy to outright handsome. "Luke Fletcher." He sticks out his hand, and I shake it.

"So you want to work with Mindy's record label?"

He nods. "I'm a songwriter."

"You've sent in your demos?"

Another nod. "Yes, but that's not generally how your sister operates."

Mindy likes to search out talent on her own. It's why she has the position she's in now at Rebel Records. She spent years wading through thousands of artists other record labels were rejecting, went to shows all over the country, offered the ones she liked exclusive rights to shop them, and discovered a knack for turning them into a success. Her first big client was a guy she found busking on a street corner who ended up opening at the Grammys after the release of his first album.

"This probably isn't the best place to pitch to her." I give him an apologetic wince. "It is a good way to get kicked out of one of these places, though. I don't know if that's how you want to be remembered."

He takes his hat off and runs his fingers through his

shaggy hair. "I don't know what else to do. I've tried every-thing. If you have any better ideas, I'm all ears."

"There you are." Mindy pushes her way between us, her gaze flicking from Luke to me and then whipping back in his direction. "Hey. Didn't you stand outside my office for hours with a boom box?"

Luke slides his hat back on, his ears going red even though he plays it smooth. "That might have been someone who vaguely resembles me."

Her hand goes to her hip. "How did you get in here?"

He attempts to charm her with a grin. "A friend invited me."

"Right."

Her expression blanks into one I find familiar. It's the same face she gave me and Taylor when we snuck out to meet boys when I was fourteen. It's the look that says, *Finley's not here, so I'm in charge, and you're in trouble.*

"This isn't how this works. You need to leave," she says.

"How does it work, then?" His hands spread in an gesture of innocence. "I would love for you to enlighten me."

"Mindy." A masculine hand comes to rest on Mindy's shoulder, right where it meets her neck. "Excuse me for inter-rupting." The interloper flashes a blindingly white smile in my direction before his head dips toward her ear. "Can I talk to you in private?"

Over the man's shoulder, I catch Luke's open-mouthed shock. I don't blame him. It's Blake Bonham, lead singer of Vacation Mustache, one of Mindy's most high-profile clients. His features aren't conventionally attractive—his nose is slightly too large for his narrow face, his dark hair flirts with his chin, his eyes are a touch too small, his mouth is a little too wide. None of it should fit together, yet he commands attention. He's over six feet tall and as broad as a tank. The whole bar area has fallen silent, staring at him.

"Fine," Mindy says.

His hand dips to her elbow as they make their way through the crowd, moving away from the bar. He's bending down, speaking in her ear.

Hm. "I'm surprised she—"

"That was Blake Bonham." Luke's eyes meet mine, and then his mouth snaps shut.

"Yeah, I know." I frown. Blake seemed awfully familiar with his hands. Possessive. Not to mention the way he looked at her, his gaze intense. And then when he leaned into her, speaking in her ear...

Is she...? No way.

Luke groans. "I acted like a total fanboy. I couldn't even speak."

I pat his arm. "You were fine." I wrinkle my nose in thought. "Isn't he married?"

"Yeah, to Jeanette Adams, the actress." His brow lifts. "Why? You interested?"

"Me? No. Just curious. He was sort of..." I take a sip of my drink, not wanting to say something personal about my sister to this stranger.

He picks up the crumbs of my thoughts anyway, his eyes turning thoughtful. "He's into her."

"Maybe." I shrug. "Is his wife here?"

"Who knows? I'll tell you one thing, though." He glances around then motions for me to come closer.

I tilt my head toward Luke, pointing my ear in his direction while my gaze moves out to the crowd of people. A familiar figure catches my eye. My heart stops, panic wrapping its hands around me in an ice-cold embrace. I catch the angle of his jaw and the sharpness of his cheekbone as the figure is spinning around to move in the opposite direction.

Maybe it's not him. It was only a glimpse. But I would recognize that profile anywhere.

Ben.

CHAPTER
Eight

I shouldn't have come. Piper is talking to a man at the bar, their heads bent toward each other. The possessiveness that bursts through me is alarming.

More of these inconvenient *feelings*. Irritated, I turn around to leave. I'll call Arnold back, have him wait outside Mindy's apartment to make sure they get home safe. Then I'll call Piper tomorrow about the studio space. No. I'll have someone else call her. I'll have an assistant of an assistant write her a note and send it via carrier pigeon.

I've truly gone mad.

The crowd parts and I nearly run into Mindy Fox, who is stalking in my direction. Our eyes meet. She's clearly agitated, her color high, her jaw hard, fists clenched at her sides.

We crossed swords the last time we spoke, in Whitby at Easter. Piper wanted to leave the small town, so I had invited her to the city. I would have given her one of the staff apartments in my building, but Mindy offered her spare room, shooting me suspicious looks that would have cut glass. Once Piper left the conversation, Mindy proceeded to tell me in graphic terms just how much she would hurt me if I did anything to cause Piper any kind of emotional distress. Her actual words were, "If you upset her, I will shove my foot so far up your ass you will choke on my toes."

I glance around for an alternate escape route. *No time.*

She stops right in my path, her hands on her hips. "Oliver. I wish I could say it was a pleasure to see you again."

"Am I that scary to you? How flattering."

"I aim to please." Her eyes are sparking with fire.

I stay silent. She's like a powder keg ready to explode. We are surrounded by temperamental artists, and I suppose working with them would drive anyone into a rage, but this is her job. You'd think she'd be used to it.

"What are you doing here, Oliver?"

"Enjoying the party." I lift a hand at the general revelry.

Her brows lift. "Are you here because of Piper?"

I tilt my head. "What if I am?"

"I don't trust you."

"That's because you have a modicum of intelligence." I keep my voice dry.

"I see the way you watch her. She's not something for you to play with. Piper is good down to her very soul. She's also trusting and innocent, despite going through hell, and somehow still doesn't recognize a snake when she sees one."

I stare at her, impassive. I'm sure she's right, but she doesn't know that I would carve out my own heart before I hurt Piper. Intentionally, anyway. Unintentional damage is another story.

She stares back at me, unwavering. "I know how men like you operate."

"You don't know anything about me."

She opens her mouth to retort but cuts off when something over my shoulder catches her attention, her gaze narrowing. "Ben." The name escapes her like a hiss.

I whip around, already on the move, scanning the crowd in search of Ben's slimy face. Mindy follows me. I stop at the edge of the dance floor. "I don't see him. Are you sure it was him?"

She's eyeing the people around us, going up on her toes to try to see over heads. "It was just a flash, but the features... it looked almost exactly like him. The hair was a little darker, but I would recognize those beady little eyes anywhere. I would cheerfully murder him."

I open my mouth to say, "Get in line," but before I can speak, Piper appears next to me, her face ashen.

"I saw Ben."

Mindy grabs her arm. "Me too. Did you see where he went?"

Piper nods, the movement robotic. "Out a side door. I didn't follow." She's shivering even though it's sweltering with all the bodies packed in here.

My fingers itch to take her in my arms and soothe her, and I clench my hands into fists. These thoughts are not helpful or normal. Not for me. They tug at the restraints I've built around my emotions. I don't have any weaknesses. I don't allow it.

Mindy wraps her arm around Piper's shoulder.

"Can we leave now?" Piper asks.

"No," Mindy says.

"Yes," I say at the same time.

Mindy glares at me and then softens her expression for Piper. "I can't leave quite yet. Let me find Ally, though, and maybe I can—"

"I'll take her home." *What am I doing?*

"No." Mindy shoots more daggers at me with her eyes.

Piper squeezes her arm. "Mindy, it's fine. I'll see you at home." They exchange a look, some wordless communication passing between them.

Mindy's mouth thins into a line, but she nods. "Fine. Text me as soon as you're home."

"Promise."

I take a few steps away and wait while Piper hugs her sister. Then we're winding through the throng, weaving around clusters of people. I glance at her periodically, making sure she's still nearby.

I've seen Piper thin and fatigued when she first left Ben. I've seen her in her pajamas, ready for bed. I saw her casual in my offices earlier this week. I've never seen her like this, wearing a dress that reveals every dip and curve, her hair pulled up on top of her head in an artfully arranged twist, exposing the delicate lines of her neck.

The sighting of Ben clearly freaked her out initially. But now the set in her jaw is stubborn and determined. We reach the front, and I motion for her to precede me toward the line of cars along the curb, resting the tips of my fingers on the small of her back, not quite touching.

Brienne is standing outside the car, and she salutes as we approach, opening the back door.

"Hey, Miss Piper. Nice to see you again."

"Thanks, Brienne."

We slide into the back seat, and within moments, we're on the road. The interior of the car is dark and quiet. The window between the back seat and the driver is shut. It smells like leather and cologne, but every now and then, I catch a thread of Piper's perfume. Something light and fresh and fleeting.

She gazes out the window. I take a slow, deep breath. Silence doesn't bother me. I can handle it better than most people. In fact, I use it habitually to gain the upper hand and get others to speak when they otherwise wouldn't. Most people can't handle sitting with someone and not speaking. Me? I'll never crack.

"Your studio is ready." *For the love of all that's holy, what is wrong with me? What is it about Piper that turns me into a nattering moron?*

Her head turns. "What?"

"Your new space. It's ready. Did you want to see it now?

You could make sure it meets all your specifications and let me know if there are any modifications required."

She stares at me, the seconds stretching between our gazes. I lock my jaw. This time, I will not blurt out my every bleeding thought.

After an eternity, she speaks. "Okay."

"Okay," I repeat.

I never repeat the last word people speak. It's a useless habit. Clenching my shut, I face forward.

Once we're in the parking garage on the bottom floor of the building, I tell Brienne we'll call her when Piper is ready to go home. Then I lead Piper over to the section of the garage that's been converted into a separate room.

"Coded entry," I tell her as I'm keying it in. "Right now it's 1010, but we can change it if you like."

"It's fine."

I push open the door and flick on the lights. She follows me inside. We stand side by side, staring at the room.

My heart thuds. "Will this suffice?"

CHAPTER
Nine

I stare, shock rooting me in place. There's so much. I mean, honestly, I sent him a huge list to delay him, but obviously, I underestimated Oliver Nichols. He really pulled together the perfect space in the smallest amount of time. He got everything I asked for and then some.

Track lights march along the ceiling, providing more than adequate illumination without being overwhelming. My gaze jumps around, not knowing where to land first. There's the workbench with tools set in neat and precise rows and the exposed concrete pad next to it where I could create something fifteen feet tall and just as wide if I wanted. There's a drafting table in the corner and a couch near the center, set on top of plush rugs that cover the concrete floor. There's a white bookshelf with paper and notepads and little containers stuffed with pencils. There's also a minifridge in one corner.

In the other corner... I suck in an audible breath. "*Lamentation*."

I walk toward the sculpture, the lights overhead warming the dark copper. I trail a finger down the curve of the arm. It's an abstract of a person about my size, a figure hunched over itself. The limbs are spindly, long, and drooped. There's a gaping hole where the central body mass should be.

Oliver stops next to me close enough that if I tilted slightly to the right, we would touch. "I thought you might like to see it again. Maybe it will provide some inspiration while you're working here. I purchased it eight years ago." His voice is a rough whisper against my sensitive nerve endings.

I nod, resisting the urge to bend in his direction. *Eight years.* This was a good sale. My first major sale. He paid well over the asking price.

The memory hits me then. He told me he had one of my pieces in LA, when we first met, the day after I left Ben. Shocked and overwhelmed by the aftermath of hurricane Ben, I didn't have the energy to ponder the statement at the time. A lot of my memories those first few days still have big blank spots.

Oliver's eyes are fixed forward, his jawline hard and smooth.

"It spoke to you?" I ask.

His chin dips in a semblance of a nod.

"Will you tell me why?"

I'm always curious how my pieces affect other people. I know how they make me feel, but to a viewer, it's always different. It amazes me how two people can scrutinize the same work and come away with completely different insights based on their own experiences and perceptions. It's part of what makes art so interesting.

I hold my breath, waiting. I won't press him to answer. It would mean so much more if he decided to tell me on his own.

"Have you ever been hungry?" he asks.

My brows lift. "Well... yeah."

His arms cross. "More than mild hunger pangs between meals. Have you ever been starving? So hungry it feels like your insides will consume themselves?"

I stare at his profile, my voice emerging, low and soft. "Does it remind you of feeling that way?"

I want to touch him, to comfort him, to take away the pain evident in the hard line of his shoulders, but I don't want to break the spell that has him opening up more than I could have imagined. I also can't quite grasp why anyone would want a reminder of what sounds like a painful memory.

"It reminds me of how far I've come."

I look back at *Lamentation*, considering his words and considering the things he isn't saying. I know little of Oliver's past. He met Archer at a camp for disadvantaged kids, so he clearly had a less than ideal childhood, but I don't know details. He's spent his adult life acquiring... well, everything.

Maybe it's because of the lack he felt in his childhood. The hunger he describes... I can't even imagine.

What happened to his parents? Did he have siblings? Who watched after him? Does the piece represent a hunger he's now trying to fill with money and possessions?

Growing up as one of six children, I can't imagine not having a large, semidysfunctional family. Of course, now I'm no longer one of six. It's been one of five since I was eighteen.

I gesture to the hole in the center. "This was my grief. How I felt after losing Aria. How it twists and shapes you, overwhelms you, and then defines you."

The grief is still a part of me. Not a day goes by that I don't think about my sister, about how I wish she was here. It's even worse when I remember Dad. The shame is too overwhelming.

As I stare at the gaping hole in the center of the sculpture, the familiar sense of loss creeps over me. It's never far away, always hovering nearby.

"I've never experienced it."

Oliver's quiet statement snaps me out of my reverie.

"You've never experienced grief?"

A shrug. "Not as you describe. 'Only people who are capable of loving strongly can also suffer great sorrow.'"

"Tolstoy."

If I wasn't so attuned to his every facial expression, I might have missed the slight widening of his eyes. I've surprised him.

"Yes," he says.

"You're saying you've never loved." I have to clarify.

"Is that so shocking?"

"Yes."

His brows dip, the movement small enough to be nearly imperceptible. "Why?"

"Well, you're not exactly a fluffy bunny, but you're not quite Satan, either."

His mouth twitches.

My heart leaps. *Did he almost smile?*

His head turns away.

I must have imagined it. Heat spreads up my face. I called him the devil to his face. "I'm sorry. That was rude."

"I don't know. 'Not quite Satan' is one of the kindest descriptions I've heard in a while."

I laugh. His head swivels toward me, an expression flashing in his face that can only be described as yearning, but it's gone before it can take root. My breath catches in my throat. It's a heady feeling, being the object of Oliver's intense focus. I wonder what it would be like to have all that concentration directed at me in bed.

My whole body heats. I haven't felt lust in a long time, but around Oliver, it's almost intrinsic. Which is why he would make the perfect rebound.

"The offer of personal security still stands."

I blink at the abrupt change in subject. "No. Thanks."

He frowns. "Are you sure? If Ben is here, following you, it could be an indication his behavior will escalate."

I fold my arms over the growing ache spreading in my chest. "I know. I'll be fine. My family has coddled me enough over the past months. I don't need anyone to watch over me. I can't let him dictate my life anymore."

It's even more than that, though. It's about retaining control over my own life, over *anything,* after living so long under Ben's thumb. I have to move on. I have to be able to take care of myself. I can't let him pull the strings on my every decision. I can't live my life in fear. Not anymore. Besides, Ben's MO is emotional abuse. He never got physical.

Oliver doesn't argue or try to convince me I'm wrong just to make a point. He nods. "I understand."

My shoulders relax, my arms dropping to my sides. He can't know how those two simple words, so easily uttered, loosen the ball of tension pressing against my ribs. For so long, I've been struggling for autonomy—for the simple ability to make choices about my own life without constant stress and anxiety.

"Thank you. I like you." The words fall out of my mouth. I wish I could pluck them out of the air and swallow them before they reach his ears, but it's too late.

His eyes widen, his mouth popping open slightly. The full-body flush condenses and then converges in my face. *Why? Why do I do these things to myself?*

His hand lifts. Slowly, the back of his fingers grazing my cheek while he stares at me like he's never seen me before. His gaze dips to my mouth.

My heart riots in my chest. *Is he going to kiss me?*

I tip forward, unable to stop, slanting in his direction like a flower absorbing the rays of the sun. He steps back, a rush of cool air moving between us. I just stop myself from continuing the forward momentum and manage to sway back without falling over.

"I'm sorry," I murmur. Embarrassment pours over my head, dousing me in heat. "Is it because of Emma?"

I had to ask. I need to know.

He frowns at me, then his voice fills the space between us, cold and impersonal as ever. "It's late. I'll have Brienne take you home."

PIPER

Mindy's apartment is dark and quiet. I set my keys down and immediately stumble over something on the floor, almost tripping onto my face. I pick up the offending item. Mindy's purse. She must have dropped it.

I set it on the entry table. *That's weird.* Mindy is all about things being in their proper order. She's constantly cleaning and straightening, adjusting her strategically placed candles, arranging her bookshelf so some are artfully placed with the pages forward instead of the spine.

I tend to be a bit more cluttered, forgetting to put my cups in the sink, leaving the throw heaped on the couch and unfolded, setting my purse on various surfaces even though Mindy has mentioned more than once it belongs on the entry table.

I make my way into the guest bedroom, my mind returning to the latest interaction with Oliver. He must think I'm a lunatic with more baggage than a fully booked cross-continental flight.

I saw his eyes dip to my mouth. He touched my face. He *must* feel this tug of attraction. It can't be one sided. At least I hope not. I'm not crazy. Maybe it's not as overwhelming for him as it is for me.

I brush my teeth and change and get into bed, my mind still swimming around Oliver and how I almost kissed him and he stepped away. My face burns. I didn't think I could be any more embarrassed than I was the other day. How wrong I was.

But he opened up. He told me a little about his dark past other than the fact that he was hungry a lot. He looked at me with those haunted, dark, *hot* eyes. He almost smiled when I called him Satan. I couldn't have imagined it.

Then again, if Regina is his type, I don't stand a chance. She's like a sleek shark, and I'm like a shivering chihuahua. Not to mention *Emma*. When I asked him about her, he basically sent me home.

That's got to be it. He's seeing someone else. Yes, he's attracted to me, but he also has morals. That makes me feel slightly better.

Or I could be completely wrong about everything and he's not attracted to me at all. He probably thinks I'm a complete moron and he wouldn't touch me even if he was single. After all, I thought I knew Ben, too, and look how that turned out.

I fall asleep, only to wake up an hour later and spend hours staring at the ceiling and tossing and turning. Eventually, sleep finds me again sometime before dawn, but I wake up only a few hours later to deep masculine laughter.

Oliver? My groggy brain tries to make sense of the sound. *Is someone here?*

Mindy's responding giggle has my jaw dropping. *Definitely not Oliver.* Mindy wouldn't be laughing if that were the case. She'd more likely be murdering.

I don't think I've ever heard such a sound emerge from her mouth. A haughty chuckle, a sarcastic snigger, maybe. But Mindy doesn't *giggle.*

Curiosity pushes me out of bed. I grab a robe and make my way to the living room. Mindy sits on the couch, her knees inclined toward the man next to her. His arm is stretched out behind her head, his fingers playing with a strand of her hair.

"Hey," I manage to get out through the shock and confusion swirling thickly in my head and surely clouding my vision.

They both turn in my direction. Mindy is wearing her sleep tank top and shorts, and Blake is in rumpled button-up shirt and faded jeans, no shoes. I'm fairly certain it's the same outfit he was in last night.

I've interrupted the morning-after coffee. Mindy's drinking morning-after coffee with a *married man.*

Mindy stands up, her face nearly scarlet. *Now she's blushing?* I've entered an alternate dimension.

My gaze flips over to Blake. He stands and grins broadly,

approaching with a hand extended. "You must be Piper. I didn't get a chance to introduce myself last night. I'm a big fan of your work."

Surprise lifts my brow even as I reach out to shake his hand. "Thank you. Um, same?"

He chuckles, and we both glance at Mindy. Her smile is still there but tighter than it was a minute ago.

She crosses her legs, waving a hand. "Blake stopped by to talk about work stuff. He was just leaving."

I frown at her. *Does she think I'm a moron?*

Blake, for his part, is unfazed. "Right. I have some other work to get to. Excuse me, ladies." He disappears into Mindy's bedroom.

"Mindy, what the hell?" I stage whisper.

She makes a throat-slashing motion, her eyes wide, her head tilting toward where Blake disappeared. "Can we talk about this after he leaves?"

I press my lips together. I don't know whether to freak out or laugh my ass off. I can't wait to give her absolute hell. *Mindy sleeping with a client—Blake Bonham, who's supposedly married?* It's so unlike her I don't even know where to start. Mindy is a rule follower. She doesn't color outside the lines. She doesn't even lie about her weight on her driver's license.

Blake emerges from Mindy's room, shoving his wallet in his back pocket, shoes now covering his feet. He bends over Mindy, his mouth close to her ear, and says something in a low rumble.

Then he straightens. "Piper, it was nice to meet you."

"You too." I wave.

Mindy follows him to the door. I move to the kitchen and pour myself a cup of coffee while straining to make out the murmured words being exchanged. The voices stop, and there's a beat of silence before the door shuts.

I sit on the couch and sip my coffee and wait impatiently then ambush her as soon as she comes back into the room. "What was that all about?"

"What do you mean?" She picks up her and Blake's cups from the table and walks into the kitchen. "Are you hungry? I'm starved."

I follow. "Don't you dare change the subject. Why was Blake here?"

"I told you. We work together. It was work stuff." She sticks her head in the fridge.

"Okay. Let's try again. Why are you screwing Blake Bonham if you work together, and isn't he married?"

She shuts the fridge and faces me, two spots of bright red flaring on her cheeks. "You don't understand."

"So explain it. I'm sure I can keep up." I step closer and put a hand on her shoulder. "Mindy. This is me. You know I won't judge you or think less of you. I love you. Besides, you can't possibly beat me or Jake for the award for worst decision-making skills utilized by a Fox family member."

She snorts a laugh, covering her mouth with a hand and giving me a stern look. "That's not funny."

"It's a little funny."

"And Taylor is worse than even you and Jake."

I firm my mouth into a disappointed line. "Mindy."

She waves a hand. "Fine, fine. Blake and his wife are separated."

I raise my hands, palms up, in my best *What the hell?* gesture. "Then why all the sneaking around and lying to your sister, who isn't an idiot, and acting like you're doing something wrong? Why not say so?"

"The media doesn't know they're separated. No one knows except him and Jeanette. And me." She blows out a breath, rubbing her face.

"Why don't they come clean?"

She turns around again, opens the fridge, and grabs a carton of eggs and some chopped veggies. "It's complicated. And it wouldn't matter. We aren't supposed to date since my company represents him. It's a conflict of interest."

I pull a pan from the cupboard and place it on the stovetop. We both stare down at it.

Mindy sighs. "It's... there's more to it. We've been playing this little dance for years."

I lean my hip against the counter. "Years?"

She nods, her lips dipping at the corners.

"Tell me everything. From the beginning."

She flips the knob to heat the pan, grabs a bowl, and cracks a couple of eggs into it with more force than is strictly necessary. "We met when he left Music City and signed with Rebel Records three years ago. He signed with us because he needed a better PR team. His last album with them didn't do great, and he got in trouble for getting into a fistfight with his drummer after one of their shows. Press started calling him a hothead and a has-been, and he got arrested for being drunk and disorderly. Shortly after that, there were rumors about his wife sleeping with a costar."

"Which one?"

"Hand me a fork, would you?"

I move back slightly to get the fork from the drawer and pass it to her.

She whisks the eggs. "You know that movie she was in with Chris Stewart—it was like *Dirty Dancing* but in space?"

I nod. "Right. I didn't see it. But I know who you're talking about." Living in LA for the past seven years, I couldn't avoid being aware of who all the A-listers were. Ben was more into the gossip than I was, though.

"The rumors were true. She did sleep with her costar. But it wasn't cheating, according to Blake, because although he's been married to Jeanette for six years, they've been separated for five." She pours the eggs into the pan.

"Why not divorce, then?"

"They're a media-darling couple. They've been able to use their relationship as fodder over the years to help fuel both of their careers. The rumors of cheating only helped her movie sell more."

I cringe. "There's no such thing as bad press."

She stares down at the eggs in the pan. "In a sense. But it's about to end. They're waiting until she wraps up her next film, then they can publicly split, and she can use the tabloid fodder when she has her press tour."

I wrinkle my nose. "It's so calculated."

She shrugs. "It's how it is."

"I guess. There is also the nonfraternization issue you mentioned."

She opens the container of mixed veggies and shakes some into a measuring cup. "Yes. Technically, I'm not supposed to date clients."

My brows lift. "Technically, could you lose your job over this?"

She lifts the edges of the omelet, tilting the pan so the uncooked parts roll to the sides. "I don't think it would come to that, but yes."

I stare at her profile. "If I didn't just watch you measure out the exact portion of perfectly sliced vegetables for your omelet, I might think you were a creature from the beyond wearing a skin suit of my sister."

She swallows, still not meeting my eyes. "I really like him, Piper."

"Clearly."

Mindy doesn't do this. She doesn't break rules, and she doesn't talk about sappy feelings. Ever. I didn't even know she had any.

"We can't tell Finley or Taylor or anyone. Promise me."

"Are you serious? Finley?"

Taylor, I understand. With all their weirdness, she and Mindy can't say hello to each other without it coming to blows, but Finley and Mindy are close, barely a year apart. After Mom took off when we were little, they were like surrogate mothers to the rest of us.

She puts the veggies in the omelet, folds it, and turns to look at me. "It's not that I don't trust Finley, but I know she'll tell Archer, and who knows who he'll tell. Everyone will promise to keep it a secret but tell someone else, and then that person will tell someone else, and then it's everywhere. The more people who know about it, the harder it is to contain. Here." She plates the food and hands it to me before cracking more eggs into the bowl.

"I get it, and I won't say anything—I promise." I grab a fork and cut into the food, propping my hip against the counter.

She gives a quick squeeze of my shoulders. "Now we need to talk about what happened last night. I checked the guest list and spoke with security, and I can't figure out how Ben got in."

I blow out a breath. "Maybe he has an amazing doppelganger?"

She huffs out a skeptical laugh.

"I know. Wishful thinking. I'm guessing he found someone, a friend or a friend of a friend, to get him a guest pass. He is well connected from selling art to celebrities in LA."

It was one of the reasons I hired him as my manager. Ben knows a lot of important people, and they all love him. To anyone who hasn't lived with him, Ben is charming, friendly, and charismatic. He's one of those people who will focus on you absolutely, making you feel like you're the center of his attention and the only one who matters. No one can resist being a little dazzled after having a conversation with him.

"Do you think we should be worried?" Mindy asks carefully, her focus on the pan.

We tried to file a police report back in LA. Emotional

abuse can be a crime in California. But it was difficult to prove because he never actually threatened to hurt me, and it was his word against mine.

After I left, Ben started a smear campaign, saying I was mentally unstable, doing drugs, and had hired someone to beat him up. It was typical Ben behavior: accuse me of doing the things he was actually doing. Deny, deflect, and play the victim.

Some people might have believed him—he did have a black eye courtesy of Oliver—but I haven't been back in LA since February, and I haven't heard of him spreading any more rumors, and it all seems to have blown over.

I blow out a breath. "I don't know. I don't think so. Maybe we should file a police report just in case? I don't think they'll do much about one package and a potential sighting. It doesn't seem to be enough to constitute stalking. But it would be nice to have a paper trail if..."

I don't want to say it. I don't want to think it. But I wouldn't be surprised if Ben's behavior continued to escalate. It always did.

"We can do it after breakfast. We'll go together." She plates her food and nudges me toward the dining table. "Come on. First, I want to hear what happened after you and Oliver left."

We sit, and I recap parts of last night, telling her about the studio Oliver put together in an astoundingly quick time, but I leave out my embarrassing behavior and our conversation about *Lamentation*. It's too personal. I listen to another round of "be careful around that guy" and "Oliver might be a megalomaniac" speeches, but I understand they comes from a good place.

As we finish eating, though, a thought sneaks into my mind, a question that I didn't think to consider until now: *Why was Oliver at the event last night?*

Eleven

Oliver

"This isn't mine." Piper crouches down next to a golden sun propped against the wall, a confused frown marring her face as she inspects it before meeting my eyes. Her brows furrow. "It has a serial number on it."

I walk over to her, my shoes tapping on the concrete floor. Squatting beside her, I examine the piece resting next to it, some kind of patterned dragonfly. "This one too? It doesn't look like you."

We're alone in the storage room in SH Kingdom, the gallery that will be opening in a few short months. I texted Piper earlier this morning to let her know the shipment of her work had arrived, even though I could have had Carson do it. She asked me to accompany her to view the pieces.

I don't know if she realizes I could never tell her no. Of

course, I am apparently capable of denying her unspoken requests when her eyes devour me like she wants to eat me. But I acted out of pure self-preservation. If I start kissing Piper, I don't think I could stop.

I should have told her about Emma. But the question came out of left field, and she had scrambled my thoughts. It wasn't until later that I realized she had likely seen Emma's texts.

"He probably bought it at Pottery Barn." She sighs.

"Why would he do that?"

She stands, wiping her palms on her jeans. "To mess with me in any way he possibly can. I've given up trying to understand anything Ben does. I don't think like a psychopath."

"It's a good thing I do." I pull my phone out of the inside pocket of my suit jacket.

Piper stops me with a soft hand on my arm. "It's okay. Don't call whoever you're calling. Then we're just playing into his hands. That's what he wants."

I blink at her. "He wants to feel the full force of my legal team?"

Ben may not realize it yet, but he's going to be ruined. I've been waiting for an excuse ever since I laid eyes on him. He's a bully, and I can't abide it.

"He wants to get a reaction. He wants the attention. He wants any kind of connection to me, to get under my skin to prove he still can. I can't give it to him. I won't. Not anymore. It's not worth it. I wouldn't have been able to use anything I made when I was with him, anyway." Her arms cross, and she gazes at the concrete floor.

"There's one more box. Should we even bother?"

She shrugs. "I guess."

I open it up with the utility knife left on the shelf and pull out a few small pieces wrapped in packing paper. The first one I unfold is a cast sculpture that resembles an Oscar except it's bronze instead of gold and the figure of the man is wearing overalls, holding a large hammer, and has a smile on his burnished face.

"Oh." Piper's voice tugs my attention. She's right next to me, peering over my shoulder, close enough for me to catch a whiff of her perfume. "I made that one for Dad when I was sixteen." Her smile is sheepish. "Best Dad award. Finley sent it to me after he passed. He kept it in the office at Fox Cottages."

I hand it to her. She hefts it up to peer underneath, rubbing a spot then frowning. "It's scratched. I wonder if he was trying to mess with it."

She sets it to the side, and then we go through the rest of the box, discarding a flower made from old spoons and a bird made from various nuts and bolts. All replicas done by amateurs.

"None of these are mine. Only this." She picks up the Dad award and smiles, but it doesn't reach her eyes. "I guess I should be grateful he sent anything at all."

I want to tie Ben up by his balls from the High Bridge and let the pigeons have at him. Instead, I say carefully, "Are you certain you don't want me to have my lawyer look into potential recourse so we can obtain your actual work?"

She shakes her head. "Don't bother. It's not worth it. I

really thought I wanted it all back, but I don't want anything that reminds me of that time in my life. I want to move on. Create something that represents who I am now. Whoever that is." She chuckles lightly.

I stare at her, wondering for a second at how she can be so vulnerable yet contain a steel core of strength. "Are you hungry?"

She startles at the abrupt question, watching me for a second before answering. "Yes."

"I know a good place nearby." I make it a statement instead of a question and then brace myself for a rejection.

"Let's do it." She immediately flushes. "I mean, let's go."

———

"A food truck? Really?" Piper's question isn't haughty or dismissive. If anything, she sounds delighted as we make our way to the end of the line.

"Everything we need is here. Lunch and then dessert." I gesture at the Salvadorian food truck and then swing my hand over to Scarlett's cupcake food truck parked on the corner.

"Sounds perfect. I love pupusas. And cupcakes." She lifts a hand to shade her eyes, squinting in the afternoon sunshine. "For Goodness Cakes," she says, reading the words on the side of the truck. "That's so cute." She scans over the rest of the outdoor seating area. "This is a nice setup."

"I know. I helped finance it."

Guy and Scarlett took our original concept of Restaurant

Row, which was a whole block of upscale dining establishments, and shifted it into something better. Guy's restaurant, Decadence, sits on the corner, open for dinner only, with an exclusive and extravagant menu he can charge out the ass for since he's a celebrity chef and entrepreneur. During evening hours, patrons can also sit outside, where the elegance continues with fairy lights and strategically placed outdoor heaters. Lunch, however, is a much less pretentious event. There are food trucks, umbrellas offer shade, and a small grassy area sports a stack of giant outdoor games for adults and children alike.

"They circulate a variety of food trucks in the space for lunch, and the truck owners are given the opportunity to host a guest menu in the restaurant to showcase their culinary skills," I explain to Piper.

"What a great idea."

I nod. I did not agree originally, but I was happy to be proven wrong.

Movement in my peripheral vision grabs my notice. Someone clutching a giant box beelines in our direction. The figure, mostly obscured by the load, approaches at a near jog. With one hand, I grab Piper's elbow to move her out of the way just in time, taking the brunt of the impact to my shoulder.

"Watch it," I tell the box-carrying pinball.

"Oh, I'm so sorry," a feminine voice calls out from behind the swath of cardboard. "I'm running late, and I can't see anything over this gosh darn—" She shifts the box to her side, and when our eyes meet, she blinks at me.

"Hey. I know you." She squints. "You're that guy with the plane."

She's in her early twenties, with dark hair, flour-dusted jeans, and a black T-shirt that reads A Vulcan in the Streets, a Klingon in the Sheets.

"You don't look familiar." I know exactly who she is. I never forget a face.

My haughty dismissal does nothing to deflect her. "We met in Blue Falls, remember? You flew down there with Guy."

"He flew with me," I correct.

"Right." She frowns. "I guess that was a couple years ago, and I'm not really one of the important people in that story."

"Fred!" Scarlett jogs toward us from the direction of her truck, her red hair tied back under a hairnet and an apron covering her petite form. "I know you have a real job now, but I needed that flour ten minutes ago." She comes to an abrupt halt a few feet away when her eyes lock with mine. "Oliver. What are you doing here?"

"Eating."

Scarlett puts a hand on her cocked hip. I'm pretty sure she hates me. It might be because she overheard me tell Guy he should "stop fucking that cupcake woman." I thought perhaps I had redeemed myself by lending my private jet so Guy could do a grand gesture that won her affections, but apparently not. Not that I care.

Fred shifts the box again. Scarlett looks between Piper and me, a groove deepening between her brows.

"I love the name of your food truck." Piper's warm voice

cuts through the strained pause in conversation. "Please don't let us hold you up from your work. We'll be sure to come over to get some cupcakes in a little bit so we can meet properly."

Scarlett's brows lift, and she smiles at Piper. "Sounds great." She grabs the box, Fred gives us an awkward wave, and they make their way back to the truck.

Piper's inquisitive gaze meets mine, but before she can ask whatever question is stewing in her mind, it's our turn to order lunch.

A few minutes later, we've retrieved our order from the window, and we make our way to a table under the shade of a silver maple tree next to an open grassy area. She sits across from me. Her hair flicks in the breeze, the sun shining on her face. She tucks the strand behind her ear, exposing the fragile shell. It makes me want to bite it.

Her eyes lift, meeting mine. She smiles.

My chest aches, and the truth hits me like a box of flour to the face. She said she *likes* me. It's unfathomable, yet I want to believe it, which is terrifying and probably means that I like her too. She hasn't quite realized I'm an absolute dick, for some ungodly reason. Once the truth comes out, she'll run screaming for the hills.

I've never done this with anyone. I've never had lunch solely because I enjoyed being in someone's company. She's comforting, like sunshine and warmth and everything I've missed in my ruthless rise to the top. I want to see what she's going to say or do next, because it's always surprising.

This isn't like me. I don't do things for joy. Everything I

do is for profit or gain. It's oddly exhilarating, especially when everything else in my life has been so mind-numbingly dull.

"What was she talking about, with the plane?" Piper spreads a napkin in her lap and picks up her fork.

I take a drink of water and pull myself together. "I helped Guy Chapman get to Texas on short notice. He owns the restaurant over there." I motion with my head before taking a bite of food. "Scarlett was parking here, preventing the owner of the parcel from selling to us. She was completely in the way of our deal. Then the idiot went and fell for her, despite my many protests. They hit a rough patch in which I was indirectly involved, so I made it up to him by letting him use my plane in a valiant effort to win her back. A success." I lift my water bottle like I'm toasting the achievement and take a sip.

She eyes me, a small smile playing around her lips. "You're quite the white knight."

I almost choke on my food. "No. I'm a self-serving prick. I helped him because I didn't want to lose my investment."

Her smile grows.

"Piper, I'm the villain in most people's stories."

"See, and I think that just makes you more interesting. But also, it's not true. Ben was a villain, and you are nothing like him."

I agree, but Ben is a weak-minded fool, whereas I'm self-aware enough to understand how my behavior is perceived by most people. "How can you be so sure?"

"You might be ruthless and direct. You might commit

morally gray behaviors to get what you want, but you also pay attention and show remarkable thoughtfulness to the people you care about."

Shock freezes me in place. *Me? Care? What in the—?*

"You treat your employees very well."

"Because I want them to work hard."

"You let Carson argue with you."

I wave a hand. "That's just basic intelligence. If you can't trust the people you hire to tell you hard truths and speak their mind, then you have no business being in charge."

"You didn't have to concede the majority stakes in the business to Finley. But you did."

I did it to get closer to Piper, and if she knew how I found the property in the first place, she might not be so ready to sing my praises.

Twelve

Piper

"Why are you looking at me like that?" I can't maintain the eye contact. Heat creeps up my neck. I poke at the last few bites on my plate with a fork.

I can't believe Oliver is eating out of a to-go carton from a food truck in a parking lot. I would have expected him to take me to one of those places where the rich and powerful go to see and be seen, with paparazzi right outside the door and plates with miniscule portions that cost three thousand dollars.

The man lives in his three-piece suit. I've never even seen him without a tie. He is always serious and fierce and threatens anyone who stands in the way of his endeavors. It's hard to reconcile that image with this eating experience. This is so... normal and lowkey for a high-powered billionaire.

Maybe I shouldn't be so surprised. He did come to our family home and decorate eggs then slept on our ancient couch without complaint. He could have left. He could have not come in the first place.

"You have a unique way of looking at things." One corner of his mouth tips up in what I'm coming to recognize is the closest he gets to smiling.

A container is slapped down on the table between to us. The young teenage girl bearing it shoots me a glance and then says to Oliver, "Hey. Scarlett told us to bring you these." She's holding hands with another teen girl, but her companion does not seem happy about it. She's grunting softly, trying to pull her hand away.

"You can let Emma go. I've got her," Oliver says.

She does and the other girl throws herself over onto the bench seat next to Oliver and immediately pats him forcefully on the shoulder and head.

Emma. The name clicks into my mind, a puzzle piece slotting together, the overall picture coming into focus.

Emma? Emma is a child?

I don't have time to process this new information.

"Who are you?" the other girl asks me.

The teens bear a strong resemblance to each other. They both have dark hair and the same heart-shaped face, but the girl smacking Oliver on the head and laughing has wider eyes and a more generous mouth.

"I'm Piper."

Oliver slides off the bench, helping Emma stand next to him. "These are Guy's sisters, Ava and Emma. Did you want to play with that?" He points at a giant Connect 4 game resting in the grass, and Emma claps her hands roughly. Then she grabs at him, rocking toward the game.

Ava follows them. "I want to do it too."

A second later, Scarlett takes Oliver's spot across from me. "Hi again! I hope we weren't interrupting anything." Scarlett's voice is sweet with a subtle drawl.

"Not at all. Thank you so much for the cupcakes. You didn't have to do that."

"It's my pleasure." Her smile is warm and bright. "I'm Scarlett Jackson."

"Piper Fox."

"It's nice to meet you, Piper." She nods to the container Ava set on the table. "It's my bestseller. It's called 'Guy Chapman is a Butt-Sniffing Douche Double Chocolate with Nougat.'"

A startled laugh breaks out of me. I peer through the clear plastic top, and my eyes widen at the frosting perfectly swirled into a rose shape. "This looks amazing. Almost too good to eat." Then I remember what Oliver told me. "Isn't Guy your boyfriend?"

Scarlett beams at me. "Fiancé." She stretches out a hand.

I lean forward. "What a beautiful ring." It's a sapphire, maybe two carats, surrounded by an intricately etched band.

"It really is." She draws her hand back and then calls out to Oliver, "Have you made a decision on whether you'll be a part of the wedding? Emma would love it if you were there, and you can bring Piper too."

He scowls at her. "I see Guy found someone even more devious than he is."

"Why, Oliver, whatever could you mean?" Her tone is all forced innocence.

Emma hands him a blue circular game piece the size of a dinner plate, and he takes it for a second then hands it back to her. She grins and dashes back to the game board.

"I haven't decided." His voice is carefully light and deceptively soft, but his jaw is hard.

Scarlett tsk-tsks. "Stop being difficult and just agree. You will eventually, anyway."

"I'm not being difficult, and I will not agree eventually, especially if you are trying to manipulate me."

She turns back to me and makes no effort to lower her voice. "Guy was cranky, too, when we first met, but underneath that hard shell is a gooey interior."

"I don't have a gooey interior." Oliver is sitting on the grass, watching the girls. His legs are stretched out in front of him, and he's propped back on his hands. The sun shines on his dark hair. His pose draws my eye to his broad shoulders and tapered waist, all of it impeccably outlined by his perfectly tailored suit.

My own interior starts to feel a bit gooey.

"You're totally a softy," Ava says. "Otherwise, Emma wouldn't like you."

Emma laughs, the sound full of pure joy. Oliver stands up, helping them stack the game pieces.

"Emma has Angelman syndrome." Scarlett leans toward me, keeping her voice low.

"What does that mean?"

"It's a chromosomal disorder. Deletion or defect of chromosome 15. It's rare, and the range of ways people are affected by it varies by subtype. She can't speak, but she does understand what we're saying. She communicates mostly through gestures—Fred's been teaching us some sign language, actually, so that's been helpful." She smiles at me, the motion lighting up her face.

"She seems very sweet." I look at Emma and Oliver. Now he's kneeling on the grass while they stack the game pieces. I need to reframe my prior thoughts on Emma. I can't believe I had jealous and bitter thoughts about a child.

"She is. Being a part of her life has been one of the most rewarding experiences. Also a little stressful at times, as you can probably imagine. It's been difficult lately." She winces. "Teenage hormones. She's been a little more aggressive, and we had to fight with our insurance to get her on birth control to stop her periods." She shakes her head with a sigh. "She needs help in the bathroom, with grooming, with getting ready, and all of that as it is. I don't know how we would have been able to explain the bleeding every month or get her to understand."

"I barely understood it when I got my first period. It was terrifying," I say.

"Right." Scarlett chuckles. "It's an awful time for all of us."

Scarlett is an amazing human, someone I would love to befriend.

Oliver, lounging in his expensive suit now covered in

grass, isn't doing much to showcase the heartless-businessman persona he was just trying to convince me of. Honestly, him trying to persuade me he's terrible just makes me like him more. Something is clearly wrong with me.

"Anyway, enough about me. Did you enjoy the pupusas?"

"They were amazing."

"On one of our first dates, Guy and I had dinner from that same truck. We have them here at least once a month now."

"Oh, this isn't a date." Except the fluttering in my stomach indicates otherwise, suggesting I might want it to be a date. I glance at Oliver, but he's busy catching the game piece Ava tosses to him like a frisbee. I can't tell if he's still listening to any of this.

Scarlett lifts her brows, saying nothing.

"We're friends" I continue. "Colleagues. I, um, Oliver and my sister own a camp together, and he's going to feature some of my pieces in a new gallery in a couple months."

"She's being kind," he says. "I bribed her into it."

So he is still listening.

Scarlett laughs. "That sounds about right. What kind of pieces are you making?"

"Metal sculptures."

Oliver interjects again. "She's an amazing artist."

Scarlett rubs her lips together. "Wow. Oliver isn't one to dole out compliments, so you must be good."

Sure. I'm great when I can actually work, but right now, I'm just the queen of suck.

"I see you've ambushed Oliver." A tall, dark-haired man in a suit and tie bends over Scarlett. "Well done."

She turns her face up, and he brushes a kiss over her mouth.

I look away, feeling like a voyeur.

"Well, asking him nicely wasn't working. Piper, this is my fiancé, Guy. Guy, this is Piper. She's Oliver's...?" Scarlett raises her brows at me.

"Piper is contractually obligated to me," Oliver says.

Guy grins at him. "That's the only reason most people hang out with you."

"Hi." I shake Guy's hand. "It's nice to meet you."

Emma comes bounding over and wraps her arms around Guy's midsection. He hugs her to him, saying something in her ear. She goes back over to Oliver and rests against him, her smile wide as he puts his arm around her.

Guy sits next to Scarlett across from me, propping his elbows on the picnic table and peering down at the cupcake package between us. "Ah, my favorite flavor." His smile is mischievous.

I tap the name of the flavor scrawled on the side. "It is named after you, I hear."

"Yep. It's how Scarlett wooed me."

She laughs and hits him gently on the arm. "It worked, didn't it?"

"Like a charm. So, Piper, you think you can convince Oliver to be in our wedding?"

I shrug. "I can try."

A second later, Oliver is standing next to the table. "I think that's our cue to leave."

Guy lifts his hands. "I just got here."

"Exactly why it's the perfect time to escape."

"I'm hurt," Guy says, but his tone is anything but.

"Are you ready? Brienne is waiting for us down the block." Oliver picks up the cupcake and holds out his free hand in my direction.

There's no way I can turn down the offer of handholding with Oliver. I let him draw me up to standing, but then he immediately releases me.

Drat. I give Guy and Scarlett an apologetic look, but they aren't bothered in the slightest. Clearly, they are used to Oliver's brash behavior.

"It was really nice to meet you," I say.

We make our goodbyes. Emma hugs Oliver. Guy shakes his hand.

Scarlett gives me a quick squeeze. "Free cupcakes for life if you can talk him into it," she says with a wink.

Minutes later, we're sliding into the back seat of Oliver's car. He directs Brienne to the West Village to drop me off first.

As soon as the car pulls from the curb, I turn to Oliver. "I saw the text on your phone from Emma last week, and I thought, I thought she was a—" I wince, not even wanting to say it. "Lover, or something. When I asked you about her, why didn't you tell me she was a child?"

His face is inscrutable. "I didn't know who you were referring to. It threw me off. I didn't know where it came from. I didn't put together that you would have seen her texts and wondered."

I guess it makes sense. I frown, crossing my arms. "Why were you at the event in Brooklyn? Were you there to see Regina?"

And the verbal diarrhea keeps on coming. It's so obvious I'm jealous. I might as well carry a neon sign around that says, "Desperate loser seeks reclusive billionaire—only Oliver Nichols need apply."

"Piper, I'm not seeing anyone." His words are impassive, his face blank.

I uncross my arms. "Really?"

"I haven't been with a woman in a long time."

My mouth hangs open. *What does he mean? How long are we talking about, here?*

His being rich, in and of itself, is enough for most women to throw themselves at his feet, but he's also handsome and mysterious. It can't have been *that* long.

"Me either." The words pop out. "I mean, not that I haven't been involved with a *woman* in a long time, but you know what I mean. With Ben and me, we didn't... that is to say, we hadn't been together for a while. Even before I left him."

Oliver doesn't say anything for a full city block. "Will you explain what you mean?" he finally asks, his voice low. "You and Ben hadn't...?"

I still can't meet his eyes. The pressure of his gaze is too much. I can't handle the scrutiny. "We hadn't slept together in over a year."

So embarrassing. Why am I telling him this? I haven't told anyone else about this, not even Taylor.

"It wasn't that I didn't want to be with him—well, I didn't really want to by that point, but after we'd been together for a year or so, he struggled to... perform. He told me it was my fault. He told me I was too cold, too unfeeling."

I risk a glance at him. His face is like stone. Very angry stone. For some reason, it gives me courage to have made Oliver angry at Ben.

"I gave all my passion to my work, and there wasn't enough left for him," I say. "That was his theory. At first, I tried, but nothing was ever enough, so after a while, it was easier to just... not. And he really didn't seem to care. He cared about perception, how things were seen by other people, but that was about it."

As the words fall out, the weight of them lifts. They are no longer wound into a hard ball in my chest. Even if Oliver says nothing, even if he judges me for all that I've shared, I feel a little lighter.

He exhales slowly, the sound winding through me. *Has he been holding his breath this whole time?*

His voice, when it emerges, is carefully controlled. "You are not unfeeling or cold, Piper. You were never the problem."

I shrug. If you're told something enough, you start to believe it. "What about you?" I ask before I can chicken out.

He pauses. "What about me?"

"Why has it been a long time for you?"

He shifts in the seat, more tense than I've ever seen him. "It's difficult to know if someone wants you because of you or only because of what you have to offer."

My earlier thought trickles back in. Women probably throw themselves at him because of his wealth. But his wealth doesn't define him as a person.

He meets my eyes, his own dark and intense. "Every woman I've dated wanted something from me, and once I provided it, or if I refused to provide it, they disappeared. My last entanglement sold me out to the press. I can't trust people."

"Same."

He sits back slightly. "We are not the same."

If his face weren't impassive as a wall, I'd think he was surprised.

"Um, excuse me. I had my entire psyche stomped on by a sociopath. I think I know if I have trust issues."

"You might have trust issues now, but you have the capacity to trust again. You're healing. You'll bounce back, fall in love with an accountant, move to Vermont, and have a litter of children and a border collie named Muffins."

I laugh. "Muffins, huh? And an accountant?"

He shifts on the seat and shrugs. "Someone nice and normal."

"Define normal. Have you met my family?"

He doesn't say anything for ten heartbeats.

"You don't think you could ever move beyond your trust issues?" I finally ask. "Find your own accountant and aptly named canine?"

The hum of the tires is quiet and soothing. The windows are tinted and dark. It's like we're in a bubble of quiet, a cozy cave.

"No. My dark places, they run too deep. I've held onto them too long."

I tilt my head, considering him. "You're right that it's different for you."

He goes still, his shoulders taut, radiating tension.

I continue, hoping he won't bite my head off. "I know what it's like to lose people. My mother walked out on us when I was young. I lost my little sister when she was only fourteen and then my father shortly after that. I thought I found love, but I never had it to begin with. And still, it's not the same. I know it's not."

I still have family. Dysfunctional as they are, they're mine, and I know they love me. I don't know all the details of Oliver's childhood, but I know enough.

"No, it's not," he says.

He's lost everyone he's ever been close to. There is no one left, and now he can't be close to anyone.

"You love Emma," I say.

"That's different."

It's interesting that he doesn't deny it.

"Why?" I ask.

"She's easy to love. She loves unconditionally."

And others don't. Others can't be trusted with his heart. Emma would never hurt him other than to smack him around a little.

"But what kind of life is that?" I ask.

Even if I made terrible decisions, even if I acted like an even bigger fool, even if I could never create again, I know I have people I love who will care about me and love me back regardless of my abilities or mistakes. I would take that over my creativity any day.

"What's the point of living?" I continue.

He glances at me. "Money. Success. Power."

Right. He hoards it all like a squirrel preparing for winter.

"The things that help us climb to the top are the same things that keep us from enjoying it when we're there," I say.

He stares ahead, his jaw clenching.

I won't let this go. I have to make him see. "You're missing what's most important when you've been shit on by life—the thing that really matters. Hope."

He faces me, his mouth twisting with skepticism. "Hope? Hope is for children who still believe in the tooth fairy."

Anger spikes into me, not necessarily at Oliver but at the people who treated him so poorly that he's lost all faith in everyone. I shake my head.

"You're wrong. You wouldn't have all that money, success, and power without it. Hope isn't some delicate, weak thing. Hope is the only thing you have left when you've been torn into nothing." My voice rises as the words spill out. "Hope is the thing that gets you out of bed and moving when you're exhausted and everything is at its darkest. Hope is what keeps you from giving up. It's being bruised and battered and torn and going on anyway. That's hope."

I'm basically yelling at him. He glares at me, his eyes burning, his hands clenched in his lap. I slump back in the seat.

"The gingko tree." His voice is gentle, subdued, a contrast to my passionate monologue.

"What?" *Will I ever stop embarrassing myself in his presence?*

"It was seen as a symbol of hope because it survived the bombing of Hiroshima."

I stare at him in confusion.

"I'm saying you're right," he says. "Hope isn't innocent or naive. Hope survives a nuclear bomb."

My pulse pounds. Ideas flicker to life inside the part of my mind that's been cold and dormant for months. My brain feels full, like something is about to be unleashed. The pressure builds, my fingers itching to create. *This is it.*

I snap back into reality. We're still driving toward Mindy's. "Wait. Can we reroute? I don't want to be dropped off at home. I need to work."

He nods without missing a beat and rolls down the window to the driver's seat, telling Brienne to take us back to his building.

Thirteen

PIPER

I barely remember the rest of the drive to Oliver's building. I go into my new room, shut the door, grab a pencil and sketchbook, and sit at the drafting table, where I stare down at the blank page. Creating is easy. You just have to take out your heart and let strangers stomp all over it.

Possibilities bubble underneath the surface of my mind, where they've been hiding under a wall of ice so thick they couldn't rise. The ice has cracked. But it's not gone.

I take a deep breath and close my eyes. The first step is always the hardest. I sketch out a few rough lines.

No. I rip the page from the book, crumple it and toss it on the floor.

Keep going.

The pencil moves across the page, hinting at jagged lines. A dove with sharp edges.

No. Another page gets tossed to the floor.

A woman. She's holding something in her hand. *A bird? A... glass object?* I hold the page up and blink at it.

No. That's not it either.

Keep going.

Three more pages end up crumpled on the floor.

The idea is there, begging to be born, but the images aren't matching the emotion I want to evoke. It's like there's this disconnect between my mind and the page. Frustration pounds through me. Another page gets thrown across the room, but the movement isn't as satisfying as I hoped.

I thought I was ready. I really thought I had it this time. But anger is a lead weight tying me down. It's like Ben is still pulling my strings.

I take a deep breath. I have to let go and let the creative process take over, like it normally does. I can't let him win.

A few hours later, I toss the pencil aside and grab my phone. I'm losing my mind. It's time for a break. I glance at the time. *Seven.* My stomach rumbles. I haven't eaten since lunch, but I need to talk to someone—to get out of my own head for a minute.

I try Finley's cell, but it goes to voicemail. We still have a landline at the house from when Fox Cottages was still in business, before Finley made the deal with Oliver to turn the property into a camp. Maybe Finley is working. She's always working.

I dial the landline while standing up, stretching my limbs, and moving over to the sofa in the center of the room.

"Hello?"

The masculine voice startles me, and I almost drop the phone. I thought I would get Finley, maybe Archer. "Jake?"

I haven't seen him since he was released from the hospital. He wasn't really in a talkative mood then, and we could barely get him to give more than one-word answers to anything.

"Hey, Piper."

This is already an improvement. Two whole words. Maybe I can get him to a compound sentence.

"You're home." I resist the urge to smack myself in the head with that Captain Obvious statement.

"I am."

There's a beat of silence, and a flare of panic spins through me. I wasn't there when he needed more. More than once.

"How is New York? Mindy?" he asks.

I sink down onto the sofa, trying to relax my nerves. He's asking me questions. This is good. He sounds good, if a little tired.

"Fine. It's fine. Mindy is fine. Everything is fine."

He might sound good, but I have clearly forgotten how to speak intelligibly. I clear my throat. *I will not say the word* fine *ever again.*

"How's Whitby?"

There's shuffling on the other end of the line. A door opens and closes as he moves through the house. I can almost smell home, roast chicken mixed with the vague scent of Pine Sol.

"Things are basically the same here as they've always been, just noisier with all the construction. Finley treats me as if I'm made of spun glass, and Archer barely lets me have more than three seconds to myself."

I tuck my legs up under me. "What do you mean?"

"He's dragged me hiking, rock climbing, and fishing. We've been bowling three times."

I chuckle. "All that, and you've barely been home a week?"

"Right? It's like I'm a toddler they're trying to wear out so I'll nap better." He releases a noisy exhalation full of frustration. "And now he said he has a surprise 'activity' for this weekend. It's all a bit... weird."

I grin at the wall. "It sounds kind of hilarious."

"I'd think so, too, if I wasn't the subject of all his attentions."

I laugh. It's almost like he's his old self again.

Jake hasn't been the same since Aria died in a car accident when they were fifteen. She was driving. Neither of them had a license or even a permit. Shortly after that, Dad got sick, and Jake helped take care of him, then Dad died too. After that, Jake went a bit off the rails. I didn't even know how bad it had gotten, not really. I was too caught up in my own life and problems. Then a few months ago, he was driving home one morning after staying up late drinking and partying with a friend, and he crashed into a tree. He broke his femur, needed surgery, and was sent into rehab facility.

And now it's almost like I have my little brother back. Almost.

"I miss you, Jakey."

His voice is gravelly when he finally speaks. "I miss you too, Pipey."

I grin at the old nickname, which Jake gave me when he was old enough to realize Jakey was a "baby name."

He takes a deep breath. "I went walking on the property today to get away from the noise and hide from Archer, and I came across that old tractor by the Carters' property line."

"Oh my gosh." I laugh, shutting my eyes, leaning my head back against the couch.

"Remember when we ran away and hid in it until after dark? I thought Finley was going to make us stay there all night to teach us a lesson." He lets out a short laugh.

"I remember."

I was eleven. Jake and Aria were eight. I convinced Aria to let me cut her hair and made a hash of it, the bangs too short, clumps missing from the back and side. Aria barely cared—she was just happy I wanted to play with her. She would have let me shave her head if I asked.

I was so sure when Dad and Finley figured out what I'd done, I would be grounded for the rest of my life, so I convinced Aria to run away and live in the tractor. Jake came with us because the twins were a package deal. We brought one bottle of water and three cookies as our only supplies and hadn't thought through any of the practical concerns, like where would we all sleep or go to the bathroom, but such is childhood.

"I love that tractor," I said. Ancient, rusted, probably a death trap but so full of character, so many various little pieces to scavenge... "It would be perfect," I whisper.

"What would be perfect? You still want to live in the tractor?"

I make a derisive noise even though I know he's just making a bad joke. "Yeah, I want to live in a tetanus-flavored hut in the woods with no windows or doors so it's extra murdery. No, you dork."

His soft laughter is everything.

I grin at the wall. "I always use recycled materials for my work, and I think some pieces of the old tractor might be perfect for one of my projects. I'd have to come see it, though, pick stuff off."

His voice brightens. "You're coming home?"

"Yeah." My mind is already sorting through the next steps needed to make it happen. Maybe it will be good to get out of the city for a couple of days. "I'll call you back when I know the details. Love you, Jake."

"I love you too."

I end the call and then dial Mindy. "Do you want to go home with me for a few days?" I ask when she picks up.

She groans. "I wish I could, but there's no way I'll have time. I'm still at work, and I'll be here all weekend. There is way too much shit hitting the fan at the moment. When are you planning on leaving?"

Someone knocks at the door.

"Come in!" I call.

Oliver walks in, carrying a covered tray. Food. Whatever

it is, it smells divine. He's still in a suit. He's removed the jacket but is still wearing the vest. My mouth waters over more than the food.

Wait. Mindy asked me a question.

I blink and avert my gaze, looking the floor. He is entirely too distracting. "Um, probably tomorrow. I'll need to see if I can rent a truck on short notice."

"A truck?" she asks.

I bite my lip, thinking, ignoring Oliver's approaching presence. "Or an SUV or something. I want to get some parts off the old tractor."

"Ah. Well, I probably won't see you, then, because it's shaping up to be a late night. But I'll try to catch you in the morning before you leave."

"Sounds good." I hang up and look at Oliver standing a few feet away, tray in hand. "Hi."

"I thought you might be hungry."

The smile tugs at my lips. "I am. We can eat it here." I pat the seat on the couch next to me.

He only hesitates a second before setting the tray on the table. Then he pulls the lid off to reveal two plates with some kind of creamy chicken, broccolini, and a dollop of mashed potatoes, along with napkins and utensils. "Why do you need to rent a truck on short notice?"

"I want to go home for a few days and harvest some materials."

Oliver hands me my plate and a fork. "We could take one of my vehicles."

"We?" I shovel in a bite of the creamy mashed potatoes.

He stands. "Do you want a drink?" He walks over to the minifridge.

"Sure. Water is fine."

He comes back with two bottles and sets them on the table within reach. "Archer asked me to come to Whitby when we spoke the other day. If you're intending on driving there as well, I have a large enough vehicle to load parts in."

I finish chewing the food in my mouth, considering him. "Okay. But I'm driving."

"That's acceptable."

I grin at him. "Road trip."

With Oliver. This should be interesting.

Fourteen

Piper

"Do you ever stop working?" We've been on the road for an hour, and Oliver has been on his laptop the entire time.

"I'm a busy man."

My eyes dip over him. I'm wearing leggings and a cropped T-shirt. My hair is pulled back into a janky ponytail. It's a three-hour drive to Whitby, and I wanted to be comfortable.

Oliver's dressed down—for him—in gunmetal-gray slacks and a black button-up dress shirt. As usual, every hair on his head is in its correct place, and his jawline is clean and shaved. Even his hair follicles refuse to defy him.

We didn't get on the road until two because of his meetings, so I spent my morning with Mindy. I showed her the Best Dad Award statue, and we decided to put it on the mantel in the living room—a high place of honor since Mindy hems and haws over every little detail in her apartment.

"Do you own any casual clothes?" I ask.

His head tilts. "Define *casual*."

"Jeans."

"Yes."

"Do you wear them?"

He taps on his keyboard for a few seconds. "Not with any regularity."

My brain conjures a compelling image of him in low-slung jeans that hug his hips then combines that with no shirt, defined chest, rumpled hair... maybe a stubbled jawline. I clear my throat, shifting in the seat. "You would look good in jeans." The murmured words fall out before I can stop them.

His fingers stop tapping.

Crap. I clench the steering wheel a little tighter. "What about sweats or track pants?"

"Yes. When I exercise."

"Do you ever wear workout clothes just out and about or when you're relaxing at home?"

Out of the corner of my eye, his head turns and his gaze hitting hits me like a caress. "No."

I switch lanes, passing a slow-moving semi, enjoying the smoothness of the ride and the easy response of the engine. We took one of Oliver's vehicles, a Cadillac Escalade that has all the bells and whistles and drives like a dream. The back could seat my entire family, which is saying something since there are a million of us.

"Don't you ever take a break?" I ask.

"Do you?"

Ha. If only he knew. I am currently in the longest, most exhausting break of my life. I would do nearly anything to get my creative juices flowing and actually get to work again. For the first time in years, though, I have hope. The thought is thrilling and terrifying. I still have to take the idea and breathe life into it, but it's got the potential to be good. Maybe even great. If I can make it happen.

Talking with Oliver helped me yank the idea out of my lifeless muse, so it stands to reason that spending more time with him might help even more. And now I know there's no Emma standing in my way. I just need to get him to agree to sleep with me. Easy peasy.

"Of course. I mean, usually even if I'm not in the studio, I'm thinking about what I'm going to work on. But metal work is what I do. It's not who I am." The words trip out of me and then hit me in the face with the truth of them.

Metal work doesn't define me. It's not the sum total of who I am. *Have I been tying all my self-worth into what I create? Is that part of the problem? When did this happen?*

Ben helped me become successful, exclusive, celebrated. He would always say how amazing I was, at first, anyway. Then his comments slowly turned, a degree at a time, until they had flipped one hundred eighty degrees. Once he flipped, he would criticize my choices and offer me his ideas to make my work better. If I disagreed, it would turn into a huge fight. When I agreed and followed his suggestions against my better judgment, not only did it leave me with a bitter taste in my mouth, but the pieces wouldn't sell. And it was my fault, according to him.

I know I can't define my personal worth based solely on my occupation. But since I haven't been able to create, I've been thinking I'm a fraud, an imposter. Maybe I took Ben's words to heart more than I realized. After all, I was making what he wanted and not what I wanted.

I need to find myself again and go of the critical voice in my mind telling me I'm not good enough, will never be good enough. That voice doesn't belong to me, anyway.

I startle back to the moment. We've both been quiet for a few miles while I dealt with my inner turmoil. *What is he thinking? Does he do the same—value himself only for his work and nothing else?*

As if he can read my thoughts, he finally speaks. "I don't think my work is who I am, not entirely."

The seconds crawl by while I wait, hoping he'll elaborate.

"Lately, everything has been a little bit tedious, and I'm not sure why. I have a diverse portfolio. I invest in a variety of endeavors, I'm constantly pursuing innovative ideas, engaging in new pursuits, and making money off all of it, and that used to be enough to motivate me. I'm busy, and yet, I'm bored."

I stay quiet, thinking. For Oliver, this was practically a monologue. *Staying busy and never having a moment of stillness is a good way to avoid dealing with any troubling thoughts or emotions.*

"Lately, it hasn't been the same. It's like I'm…" He glances out the window and then back at me. "Uninspired."

"I know exactly what you mean." I remove my foot from the gas, slowing down the vehicle as we approach Whitby proper, population 1,803.

My gaze trails past the familiar buildings—the barn-shaped hardware store, Sweet Cheeks Bakery, the Whitby Grill, and the one and only grocery store. On the other side of town, the buildings thin out, and towering pines line the road. We pass Veronica's bar, where only a few vehicles are parked in the lot. From here it's only a couple miles to Fox Cottages. Although I suppose it isn't called Fox Cottages anymore since Oliver bought it.

"What drew you to Whitby, to this area, for your camp?"

He closes his laptop and slides it into his briefcase. "I'd had my eye on this area for a long time."

He isn't really answering the question. *Interesting.*

"How long?"

He hesitates. "Eight years."

Eight years. He bought my first sculpture eight years ago. Around the same time, he started creeping around little old Whitby middle of nowhere for his camp. A camp he fought for, purchased multiple parcels of property around, then begged, pleaded, threatened, and cajoled. He eventually sent in Archer as his henchman to convince Finley to sell to him.

Quite a coincidence. The thought, once it wiggles into my mind, digs in with hooks and won't leave until I know the truth. "Was it because of me?"

I turn off the main road, following the hard-packed-dirt

drive up into the area formerly known as Fox Cottages. Heavy equipment rests silently off to the side. Piles of dirt and material sit where there used to be a road to the rental cabins. I guide the vehicle in the other direction, pull up and stop in front of the main house then put the car in park.

"Not entirely," he finally answers.

Before I can formulate any follow-up questions, an excited shriek grabs my attention. Finley bolts down the porch steps, Archer behind her.

Fifteen

OLIVER

The exterior of the Fox family home hasn't changed much since my last visit. It still looks as if the Winchester mystery house had a baby with a log cabin and the doula was a blind lumberjack. We've pulled up in the front of the building, where the main office is. It's basically a large front room connected to the residence behind it by an interior door.

The porch is freshly painted and has decidedly less sag to it than it did at my last visit, but the mess of a structure behind it is still an odd mixture of architectural styles, as if different hands have been adding to it over the years and the result is something that was supposed to be charming and ended up more like a misshapen mess.

The second Piper slides out of the driver's seat, Finley hugs her, and they commence an inexplicable ritual of affectionate gestures combined with overly loud chattering. I make my way to the rear of the vehicle to retrieve the bags.

Archer gives Piper a hug and then jogs over to me as I push the button on the trunk. He slaps me on the upper back. "Hey, man. Glad you could make it. Hungry? You're right on time for dinner. We're making tacos."

I glance at Piper as Finley ushers her inside. "Yes. Dinner would be fine."

"Here, I've got this." He takes Piper's bag from me. "Did you want to stay here or in one of the completed cabins? We only have the one free room since Jake's home, so you'd have to sleep on the couch again."

I hold back a grimace. The only compelling argument for staying here involves the possibility of Piper joining me on the monstrous couch, but after our conversation in the car, the outlook isn't good. *What if she's angry? What if my slightly obsessive—okay, very obsessive—personality scares her away?* A separate accommodation is for the best. It shouldn't affect me in the slightest.

"The cabin will be sufficient."

"Great. I'll show you where it is after dinner."

I shut the trunk, leaving my bag for now, and follow Archer up the steps and into the house. We go through the office and end up in the open dining and living area. Archer jogs up the staircase on the left to deposit Piper's bag in her room.

I stand next to the oversize dining table, glancing around as Finley and Piper are talk in the kitchen, through an arched doorway and out of sight. The Foxes have done a little bit of work. The floors appear new, shiny golden maple, but the horrid couch is still present, along with the ancient wood paneling and plethora of family photos cluttering the walls. I'm not sure if I should sit down somewhere else, go to the kitchen, or wait here for Archer.

Before I decide what to do with myself, Finley's voice gets louder, and she stalks into the dining area, grabs my shoulder, and gives me a side hug. "Hey, Oliver. Thanks for coming."

I freeze. She's never hugged me. She barely tolerates me.

I pat her shoulder once.

She releases me on a squeeze. "Jake's manning the grill," she says, pulling Piper toward the door that leads from the kitchen to the side entrance. She calls out behind her. "Will you set the table? The plates are in the cabinet by the fridge, and the utensils are in the drawer underneath." Then the door shuts, and I'm alone.

At least I have a task. I make my way to the kitchen. The countertops are new—white-and-gray-speckled granite—and the ancient fridge and oven have been replaced, but the dark wood cabinets are the same, their style dating from around 1986. I swing open the cupboard next to the fridge and grab a stack of mismatched antique plates, some of which are chipped. They need new dishes, clearly.

"Hey." Archer appears behind me, opening the fridge and stacking containers, a bowl of grated cheese, another of chopped tomatoes, and a third with shredded lettuce. "Thanks for your advice with Jake. I'm glad you came. I ordered the stuff you recommended, but I might need you to help get him into it." He glances at the door, keeping his voice low even though the sounds of Piper and Finley laughing and talking with Jake filter in from outside the door.

"What stuff?" I count out the plates and then open the drawer and stare into it. "Do we need utensils for tacos?"

"The cross-stitch thing. And no. Just grab a couple of spoons for the toppings."

*Cross-stitch? Oh, right. Carson. Cross*Fit. *Hmm.* I'm not quite sure how to break it to him.

The door opens, and the siblings march in, raising the volume in the room by at least ten decibels. Jake brings up the rear with a tray of steaming meat, filling the kitchen with the heady scent of spices and grill smoke.

Finley barks out orders like a drill sergeant—or someone who raised a brood of children. "Let's put everything on the dining table to pass around. Piper, will you help Archer grab the fixings? I'll get the tortillas."

I head into the dining room with the plates. The next few minutes are a study in organized chaos as everyone steps around the mammoth-sized oak table. Jake sits at the head, Finley and Archer on one side, and Piper on the other. I take the seat next to her.

"Are you going out to the tractor tomorrow?" Jake asks Piper, passing her the platter of chicken.

She nods. "After breakfast."

"I'll go too," Finley says, filling her taco with steak.

Jake reaches across the table for the container with the shredded cheese. "I can come with you."

Archer clears his throat. "We already have plans for tomorrow, with Oliver. I told you about it last night."

Jake gives him a blank look and then diverts his gaze to Finley. "If I shake a can of pennies at it, will it stop?"

"If you could afford a can of pennies, I might be worried," Archer shoots back.

Finley laughs.

Jake grumbles. He grabs a piece of steak from the platter and pops it in his mouth.

Archer dips his head and whispers something in Finley's ear, his hand on the back of her chair. She puts her hand on his cheek.

Piper catches my attention. "Do you want carne asada or chicken?"

I meet her questioning gaze and get lost in it.

"Oliver?" She lowers her voice, moving in close enough that our shoulders brush.

I find my voice. "Chicken."

She passes me the platter.

I fill my tortillas, my mind stuck for a second on the casual yet intimate touch of Piper's shoulder against mine. Then it goes back to the interactions at the table. The quips and the teasing, the intimate touches.

Archer and I were the same before—we were both alone. But now he has a real family. He fits somewhere, with someone.

I sort of gleaned this at Easter, but it hasn't really sunk in until now. This isn't just a messy, chaotic, mismatched house. This is a home.

I keep my expression carefully blank while an unfamiliar yearning burns a hole in my gut. *Fucking feelings.*

"How is Mindy?" Finley directs the question to Piper, shaking hot sauce on her taco. "I tried to call her the other night and she never called me back."

Piper reaches for the bowl of chopped tomatoes. "You know Mindy. She's been really busy. I barely see her. She's working too hard. All that normal, totally boring stuff." She suddenly becomes very interested in the pattern on her plate. She's hiding something.

Finley finishes chewing her bite of food, nodding. "She's always been such a hard worker, so motivated and ambitious."

I frown. *How do they not notice?*

Finley gestures in Piper's direction. "You've been busy, too, right? How is work going on the upcoming gallery exhibit?"

Piper's hand on the table flexes. "It's going great."

"Yeah?" Finley asks.

Piper takes a bite of her food instead of responding. Finley and Archer exchange a glance. Even Jake looks up from the head of the table, where he's been quietly stuffing food in his mouth.

I don't know what compels me to enter the conversation. All I know is I don't like Piper being tense. I don't like that she might be upset with me due to our earlier conversation, and I know she's hiding two secrets, one about Mindy and the other about her work. I knew something was wrong when she first came to see me about her work space, and I have yet to set eyes on any pieces she's finished for the exhibit. Clearly, she's behind schedule.

I couldn't stop myself from helping her any more than I could stop breathing. "She's been working in the studio I had built for her in my building. Piper will be the only metal sculptor we'll have at the exhibition. We were able to obtain other works, different media types, from Ariana Richards, Cat Wiant, and Beatriz Milhazes."

Every gaze at the table shifts to me.

Jake leans back in his seat. "What in the actual Daddy Warbucks name-dropping was that all about?"

Piper laughs, covering her mouth with her hand. "Daddy Warbucks?"

"He did sort of adopt us, in a sense." Finley grins at me.

Archer's brows dip together. "You are not my daddy, nor will I ever be referring to you as such."

"I think he's more of a Christian Grey type," Finley says.

Jake frowns. "Who?"

Piper cracks up, a sound so infectious I almost smile. Almost.

I push my mouth into a flat line. "I am not any type. I am solely myself."

Piper nudges me with her elbow, still chuckling. "Ain't that the truth."

Everyone laughs and continues eating, the topic switching to plans for the weekend. The conversation flows around me. *Were they teasing me?*

The earth shifts beneath me, knocking me off kilter. I

don't know what to make of it. The sensation is bewildering and enticing all at once.

Perhaps I could fit somewhere too. But I don't trust the emotion. Experience has taught me to never get too close to anyone and never place any of my hopes on the actions of other people. They always let you down.

CHAPTER

Sixteen

Oliver

The sun has set, and the sky is a dark tapestry speckled with stars by the time Archer drives me over to the cabin where I'll be sleeping. The headlights of the golf cart bounce over piles of lumber and brick and bags of concrete wreathed in shadows. He points out the various projects in progress as we pass, at least as much as we can see by the light of the moon and the cart's lights.

The existing buildings that used to be leased out to private renters are being gutted and remodeled with bunk beds for the campers and will house eight kids per cabin. Finley and Archer have built a few brand-new one- or two-person structures as private spaces for the instructors and counselors. Firepits are scattered throughout, along with picnic tables and two outdoor grilling areas with seating—a large one placed strategically in the space between the kids' cabins and a smaller one near the cabin I'll be staying in for the weekend.

"It's fully furnished," he says, flicking on the lights as we enter the A-frame. It opens directly into a living area, with a kitchenette off to one side. "The sleeping area and the bathroom are upstairs." He motions to a circular staircase leading up into the open loft.

It's small but functional. You can see part of the bed from the entryway. The walls are a neutral pale blue, and the ceiling has exposed beams in warm browns. In the kitchenette, the counters are granite and the appliances new. I put my suitcase down, and Archer hands me the key to the front door.

"Thanks for driving me over," I tell Archer.

It was easier to leave my car up at the main house and have him drive me, using one of the golf carts, since he would have to show me where to go anyway. This way, Piper can use my vehicle or put any work items she needs into it while we're here.

"No problem. We'll see you for breakfast at eight. It's going to be a busy day. Dress casual." He grins and then leaves with a wave, jogging down the porch steps and over to the golf cart.

I bring my suitcase up the stairs and open it. *Casual.* I brought chinos. That will have to do. I grab my small bag of toiletries, razor, shaving cream, and other travel-sized necessities. The bathroom is entirely white and clean, with a walk-in shower and pedestal sink with no counter space and—I glance at the empty rack—no towels.

I sigh. My phone rings. I move back into the bedroom and set my bag on the narrow dresser.

"Carson," I answer on the second ring.

"Good evening, sir. I'm calling to check in before I head out for the night."

I look at my watch. It's past eight. "You're still working?" He's normally able to leave by five.

"Just had some things to clean up and wanted to give you the status before I leave the office."

I sit on the edge of the bed. "All right. Go on."

He rattles off a list of action items I gave him that he has completed. "I pushed back all your meetings until eleven thirty Monday morning, so you should be clear for the weekend."

"Has Arthur checked in?" I ask.

"Yes, sir. No sign of Ben."

"Good." Even though I plan on spending the entire weekend with Piper, I want him to be on the lookout for Ben lurking around Mindy's apartment.

Carson is as thorough and proficient as ever, but his voice sounds... off. It's missing his normal spark. He's monosyllabic and not like his normal flashy self. I almost end the conversation there—after all, it's none of my business—but something stops me.

No, some*one* stops me. Piper. In my head. Telling me I care.

"What's wrong with you?"

Hmm. Perhaps I could have taken a more sensitive approach.

"I'm fine. It's nothing."

"You're distracted."

"It's nothing that will impact my job performance, I assure you." He takes a small breath. "Is there anything else you need?"

"No. But…" I don't know quite how to proceed. If it's a personal matter, it's not my place to interfere. "If you need anything, anything at all, you can always ask me. It doesn't have to be about work."

There's a slight pause, and when he speaks, his voice is marginally less stiff. "Understood, sir."

We hang up. I toss my phone onto the bed and then scrub my hands over my face. *What is wrong with me?*

A tentative knock at the door jerks me to my feet. I jog down the stairs. Piper is on the porch, a canvas bag in her hand.

"Hi." She lifts the bag. "I brought you some towels and things. Finley remembered there were some missing touches in here. Can I come in? I wanted to talk to you about something."

I glance behind me. The bed is upstairs, but there's a perfectly serviceable sofa right here. Images of me and Piper on couches are harmful to my willpower.

"Why don't we sit on the porch?" I take the bag from her and set it on the floor. Then I step out into the night, shutting the door and engulfing us in darkness.

She doesn't step back to accommodate my forward

motion. Her chest is only an inch from mine, her features shadowed. My pulse throbs.

After a beat, she turns away, plopping into one of the Adirondack chairs.

"What did you want to talk about?" I sit in the seat next to her.

"Well, first I wanted to apologize for all the teasing at dinner."

"It's fine. I was here at Easter, remember? Your family is very... robust."

She huffs out a small laugh. "That's a diplomatic way to put it."

"How would you put it?"

"Chaotic."

I incline my head. "That too."

She takes a deep breath and sinks a little farther back in the chair. I mimic the movement, filling my lungs with the cooling night air, breathing in the aroma of soil and pine. The light from the moon and stars overhead barely reaches us in the shadowy recesses of the porch. Over by the tree line, faint glowing dots appear and disappear. Fireflies. I haven't seen any in years, not since I was a child.

"How much did I have to do with you pursuing this property?"

Piper's low-pitched question tugs me out of my meandering thoughts. I'm not going to lie to her. I can't. If it means she avoids me from now on, so be it. That might be for the best anyway.

"After I purchased *Lamentation*, I wanted to acquire

more of your work. This was your last known address. When I saw the size and location, I wanted it." I drum my fingers on the armrest.

"So, initially you only wanted more art, but then the property happened to suit your needs?"

I stand up and move over to the porch railing, my attention on the glowing bugs in the distance. "The location and size were ideal for my needs. The fact that it was connected to you made it even more compelling."

Might as well tell her. Better to scare her away now rather than later.

The porch creaks, the air stirring at my back. She rests her hands on the railing next to mine. "Why?"

I need more time to consider my responses. "Why what?"

"Why would I make it more compelling?"

I take a deep breath and blow it out slowly, my resolve fleeing with her nearness. "I don't want to frighten you."

"It doesn't frighten me." She covers my hand where it's clenched on the patio railing. "Is it the same reason you showed up at that event in Brooklyn?"

I don't quite compute the question, at first, distracted by her touch. "What?"

"You never explained why you were there. You have your hands in a lot of things but not anything Mindy's connected to."

Shit. I can't tell her I'm having her followed and that I knew Ben would be there because the PI I hired saw him enter the event. But I don't want to lie, either.

"Oliver, you can tell me. I care about you."

My heart tumbles. "You shouldn't. I don't know how to care back."

When you grow up without something, the lack of it is always with you. I don't want to explain to Piper the irrefutable fact that I've reached thirty-five without ever being in a real adult relationship. I've outright avoided them. Regina was the only association that lasted longer than a month, and when she talked to the press, I was relieved to have an excuse to break it off.

Piper pulls her hand back. "That's not true."

"You've extolled my virtues before, but the things you think are generous are, in fact, mercenary. I make decisions to get what I want. I'm incapable of true affection."

"Come on, Oliver. We slept together." She pauses into a weighted silence. "You know what I mean—we slept next to each other. We cuddled. Pretty sure that's affection."

"I'm not a cuddler." *Not with anyone else.*

"You were with me."

I can't refute it. "I wanted to see you." I swallow. "There you have it. That's the answer to both of your questions, both times. Do you have any more?"

She shifts inexorably closer. Her mouth opens and then closes. I can almost see the thoughts scrolling through her head. She wants to know more. She wants me to expound, but I won't. I can't. It's too much. She's not ready.

"Maybe you don't think you're capable of caring for someone, but would you be willing to try?" The heat of her fingers reaches my skin through the fabric of my shirt.

"What does that mean? Try what?"

"We're friends, right? Maybe we can be friends with... extras?"

My whole body tightens with visceral need. She can't know what she's offering. It's like flying. It's beautiful and terrifying—freedom and fear in the palm of her hand.

"What precisely does 'extra' entail?"

Her fingers flex on my arm. "You know what I mean."

"Maybe we should discuss the exact parameters of your offer."

"Do you need a contract in writing?" she asks.

The thought has merit. "I'm intrigued."

She chuckles, the sound low and warm. "You would be."

The corner of my lip twitches, and her eyes dip to my mouth. My need to accept what she's offering is a primal, howling force. I want it more than I want my next breath.

But I also don't want to be some temporary fling. I crave her as much as I fear her. I don't want her to see inside all my dark spaces and find me lacking.

"You don't know what you're suggesting."

She pulls back, her hands on her hips. "I know exactly what I'm suggesting. I'm not an idiot, Oliver."

Surprised at the vehement response, I try to read her face in the dark. "I'm not rejecting the offer."

"You aren't?"

As if I could. I can tell myself that I have a choice, but I don't. I never have. Piper isn't merely a choice—she's an absolute. "No. But I have a question for you as well. Why me?"

"What?"

"Why me? Why do you want the 'extra' with me?" She could choose anyone.

She ducks her head. "We're attracted to each other. You can't deny it."

No, I can't.

She wraps her arms around her middle. "You're the only person who understands—who I *thought* understood, anyway. Ben isn't just the last person I was with—he is the only person I've been with. I can't shake the feeling that I'll never be able to move on, to move past what he put me through. I'm not asking for anything serious."

I frown, agreeing with her words yet finding them distasteful. "So what you're suggesting is a rebound?"

She nods. "So to speak."

I don't know how I feel about the word *rebound*. It leaves a bad taste in my mouth. "What does that mean? One night?"

"I don't know," she whispers. "It means whatever we want it to mean."

I want it to mean more than it implies.

"Just think about it." She fidgets, shifting on her feet. "I'll see you tomorrow."

Before I can come up with a response that will get her to stay, she's jogging down the steps and disappearing into the night. I should tell her no, tell her to find someone else, but the thought of her rebounding with anyone but me is intolerable. It's too late to run. She's crawled into the dark space in my chest and struck a match.

Seventeen

PIPER

Using a cordless drill, I remove a bolt and toss it into the old red rider wagon on the ground.

"Hey, look," Finley calls out. "This doodad came right off. You want it?"

Hanging onto the doorway of the old tractor with my elbow, I lean outside to peer at where she's crouched next to the tire, holding a lug nut.

"Sure. Toss anything you can get off in the box. I'll go through it later."

I sit back in the seat, gazing out the windowless cab, taking in the roll of the hills surrounding me. It's midmorning, the sun ascending into a bright-blue sky fringed with trees surrounding the little clearing where we've stopped amid the tractor rubble. Shutting my eyes, I take a deep breath of fresh mountain air.

"You know, you could stay here instead of going back to the city," Finley says.

"I like the city. Besides, you have so much going on. It's better I'm out of the way."

"You're never in the way. And the city might have amazing restaurants, eclectic culture, and exciting night life, but we have old rusty pieces of construction equipment and feral racoons."

I laugh. "Mindy needs me more than you do. Someone has to be there to make sure she eats and sleeps and spends at least a fraction of her time not working."

Although Mindy does have Blake now. Maybe she'd prefer me out of the way. I texted her this morning, but I haven't heard back.

We continue to work. The occasional bird call, the buzz of cicadas, and the plunk of items falling into the wagon act as the soundtrack of the morning.

"How has it been working with Oliver?" Finley calls out.

"You tell me."

Another clunk. "It's been good, actually. He's growing on me."

"Really? Me too." *In more ways than one.*

"Is that so?"

I bang on a rusty bolt with the hammer and then stop to speak. "We've been spending a lot of time together lately, and he's not quite the cretin most people think he is."

"I agree."

I tilt my upper half out of the cab of the truck again. "Really?"

She stands, wiping her hands on her jeans. "Well, it might not be my place to say anything, since it's none of my business and you're an adult and all."

I shrug. "You're an adultier adult. And none of that has stopped you from speaking your mind before."

She walks over to stand in front of me. "He's not a bad guy. But he might not be capable of love. He's never experienced it."

I feign nonchalance. "I don't know what you mean. We're just friends." But my heart twists at her words. They're too similar to what he said. Maybe they're true.

Her brows lift. "Friends? Are you sure?"

"Maybe it's more than that, but you don't need to worry. I know what I can handle, Finley."

She props a shoulder against the door of the cab, moving a little closer. "I know. I trust you to know what you need. I'm doing this thing where I'm trying to let go and not control everyone. But it's hard. You deserve the best in the world. I worry about your tender heart. I get Oliver more now. I understand him. But that doesn't change the fact that I love you, and I worry he doesn't have enough to give you what you need."

I pick up a screwdriver I set on the seat and rub the hard metal with a thumb. "He's not like Ben."

"No. He's not. I know he's not. Ben was small. He was a worm. Oliver is larger than life. Ben was a bully. Oliver isn't a bully, but he doesn't know how to be soft." She wrinkles her nose. "He's all jagged edges and money clips and perfectionism."

He's soft with me. "I wanted to see you"—I smile at the memory. Lord, how I wanted to ask some follow-ups to that one, but I won't do that yet. He's not ready.

"I think he's more than that."

She nods, considering me. "Just be careful."

"I will."

Finley pushes off the tractor and disappears under the hood, poking around in the engine bay. "Has Mindy said anything to you about Taylor?" she calls out.

"Nothing good."

She bangs on something for half a minute. "I hoped things would have improved by now. They were at least civil to each other when Jake was in the hospital. I guess it didn't last."

I remove another bolt and chuck it into the wagon. "Do you know why they're fighting?"

"Nope. Do you?" She drops more pieces onto our stack and then stops in front of me again.

I shake my head. "No. I've asked Mindy a few times, and she won't give more than a vague answer, so I stopped probing." I shrug. "You know how she is."

"How they both are." Finley leans in, holding herself up with a hand on the side of the machine. "Or should I say, how we all are. We've been through a lot, all of us, but we don't really share with each other or ask for help when we need it."

I shift in the bucket seat, turning to face her more fully.

"It could be our family motto: 'Buck up, rub some dirt in it, and then crack a joke to mask all the deeper feelings.'"

"I'll have it engraved over the door." She reaches over and touches my knee. "Really, Piper, I'm so grateful you called me when you did. That takes strength."

I duck my head. We did talk in the aftermath, when I was staying with Finley and Archer, but it never got very deep. She had all the Ben highlights. After all, she came with Archer and Oliver to rescue me. She knew I was struggling creatively before I left Whitby, but she doesn't know I'm still fighting. She doesn't know how guilty I've felt about everything she shouldered alone. Up until recently, I could hardly decide what to cereal to eat without having a meltdown, let alone confront any lingering guilt about what I had missed because of my poor choices.

"I should have left him sooner. I shouldn't have let him control my life. I'm sorry I didn't know about Jake. I'm sorry I wasn't here. I wasn't paying attention to anything but my own little bubble."

I need to talk to Jake about it too. It wasn't only Finley who suffered when the rest of us bailed.

Finley climbs up into the machine and sits in my lap, wrapping her arms around my shoulders. "I was doing the same thing. I just kept focusing on work, ignoring the growing problems and trying to pretend everything was fine."

"We're a pair of idiots."

She snorts out a laugh. "We can add that to the family motto. I'm sorry I didn't say anything before."

"I wasn't ready. This is the perfect time." I hug her back, resting my head on her shoulder. She smells like familiar laundry detergent mixed with mountain air. She smells like home. I lift my head. "I want to be here more for you and Jake. Please tell me if you need me for anything, even if it's only to unload. I'm strong enough now—I promise."

"I know you are. You called when you needed me, even though I know it's easier to stick your head in the sand and pretend like it's all fine when it's not. Asking for help is hard, but we all need a hand up sometimes. I had learned that lesson with Archer."

I laugh. "You asked for help, or Archer magically appeared and provided it despite your formidable resistance?"

She groans covering her face with a hand. "That's basically our love story." She blows out an annoyed huff. "I'm like Cinda-freaking-rella. And Archer was my fairy godmother." She wiggles her eyebrows at me. "My sexy godmother."

I snort. "What does that make me?"

She winks. "Beauty and the Beast, I'm guessing."

I chuckle. "I did sacrifice myself for your benefit, and Oliver *is* always trying to get me to stay in his enchanted castle."

"See? There you go. Next thing you know, you're being seduced by a singing candelabra and a giant library with one of those rolling ladders." She climbs off my lap and jumps down off the tractor.

I follow her out. "I've always wanted one of those. I just

hope he never turns into a prince. The Beast was way hotter."

She kicks the wagon. "You think we got enough?"

The box is over nearly full of various parts and pieces, including the steering wheel and three different knobs from the interior.

"Yeah. I think we're good for now."

We walk back along the path, dragging the wagon of goodies behind us. Leaving the parts from the tractor over by the garage-shed, we enter the main house from the side door.

Jake's voice carries into the kitchen from the living room. "Will you pass me those scissors?" There's a pause, and then he speaks again, "I think you pulled the thread too tight there."

"Would you quit looking over my shoulder?" Archer returns.

Finley and I share a confused glance. I follow her into the living room. Archer and Jake are on the couch, and Oliver is on the recliner. All three of them are holding white fabric set in embroidery frames, tugging needles through the material.

"What are you doing?" I ask.

Oliver freezes, his gaze slicing to mine.

Jake cuts at his thread with a small pair of scissors. "We're sacrificing kittens to Beelzebub. What does it look like we're doing?"

Archer keeps sewing. "We're cross-stitching."

"It's kind of lame but also kind of fun. See." Jake turns his so I can see it.

I read out loud. "Archer has a little pen..."

He turns it back around. "Well, it's not done yet. Just need two more letters."

Finley puts her hands on her hips. "Really, Jake?"

"It's cool," Archer says. "Mine is gonna say, 'Oliver is a dickass.'"

Oliver pauses in his stitching, lowering the frame to his lap, his brows drawn together. "A dickass?"

"Yup. You're kind of a dick and kind of an ass. It's the perfect insult." Archer lifts both hands like a showman revealing the word in lights on a billboard. "Dickass."

Oliver nods as if this all makes perfect sense.

Finley rests her hip against the sofa next to Archer, laying a hand on his shoulder and peering at Oliver. "I suppose you have some insulting stitching going on too?"

"No. I'm making a bird."

Everyone stares at him.

Jake leans over, trying to get a peek. "Let's see it."

Oliver inspects it briefly before turning the loop around to face us. "It's not quite finished."

It's a bluebird. The head is complete, the body about halfway done, but the stitching is neat and tidy. He's used various colors of blue so it's shaded, almost like it's ready to jump off the fabric.

"How did you...?" Jake scratches his head.

Archer laughs. "Is there anything you can't do?"

"No. I'm very good at everything." The words are delivered without emotion.

"He's not lying." Archer sets his cross-stitch to the side.

"We did archery during summer camp, and Oliver hit the bullseye almost every time."

Jake releases a beleaguered sigh then sticks a hand out toward Archer. "Would you ladies quit flirting and pass me the pink thread?"

———

I can't sleep. Again. I went to bed a few hours ago then woke up in the middle of the night when my phone chimed once, then again, then multiple times, one ding after another.

I miss seeing you.

Where did you go?

Are you with him?

I can't stand the thought of another man touching what's mine.

Chilled, I screenshot everything and then block the number. One more piece to add to the growing evidence pile, not that the cops will do much about creepy texts.

Ben must be watching the apartment. But who is this "him" he's referring to? He can't know I drove here with Oliver, since Oliver has never been to Mindy's apartment. Maybe he's guessing, trying to get a reaction. I'll have to text Mindy in the morning and tell her to be extra cautious.

Frustration boils in my blood, simmering in my veins. I wish Ben would just disappear, leave me alone, but I doubt he will. He can't handle that I left him. He wants to have the last word to show he's the one in charge. Maybe I should listen to Oliver and hire a security guard, but... I can't let Ben control my life forever.

Now I'll never fall back asleep. I shake my pillow, punch it a couple times, and flop over onto my side. The house is still and quiet. Maybe I should get up. Go downstairs, grab some water or tea.

Or I could walk right out the side door and make my way down to Oliver's cabin. It's not far. I could be there in less than five minutes. My skin prickles. He's probably awake.

He never responded to my proposition. I told him to think about it, but we haven't been alone since last night. We could be alone now, though.

What if he says no? My stomach drops.

What if he says yes? The thought is almost as frightening.

I thought I wanted a rebound, but I don't think Oliver is someone I could bounce away from. He's already burrowing his sneaky way into my heart. It's too much, too soon. I fell for Ben quickly too. I was consumed by him, and then he chewed me up and spit me out. Maybe Finley and Mindy are right. I give too much, and then I lose myself in the process.

I get up and grab my robe. I'll go downstairs. Have some water. Then I'll try to sleep.

The hallway is faintly illuminated. I stop next to the glowing night-light and sink down on my heels, brushing a finger over Minnie Mouse's fading ear. It was Aria's. When she was five, she insisted on moving it from her room to the hallway because of Jake. He always had to pee in the night, and he was scared of the dark. It probably hasn't moved since.

I stand up, take a step, and almost scream at a dark figure looming in the open doorway to Dad's room. "Jake. What are you doing?"

The door being open is shocking in and of itself. We like to keep the door shut on the past, both literally and figuratively. He rests against the frame. His arms are crossed while he gazes into the room.

"I couldn't sleep, so I was"—he gestures to the empty room—"thinking."

I stop next to him and face the room. Moonlight streams in through the double windows, illuminating the neatly made bed, a paperback resting on the nightstand, and the old green lamp on the dresser. The digital alarm clock glows with pale-green numbers, 12:27. It feels as if Dad could walk through the door any minute, lie down, and go to sleep. Like we're just waiting for him.

I glance at Aria's bedroom door obscured by the shroud of darkness and shut tight. It's probably much the same way. Like a shrine. A tomb. *When will we move on? Can we?*

Guilt grips me in a choke hold. I don't know what to say. I wasn't here when Dad died. Jake and Finley bore the brunt of everything—the aftermath when we lost Aria, Dad's illness and passing. The whole thing is a big blur for me. Unfairly so.

Jake must be thinking along the same lines. When he finally speaks, his voice is low and soft. "When he was sick, it was hard, but..." He lifts his gaze to the ceiling. "It kept me from thinking too much, from feeling too much. There was always something to do. I had to take care of him. He needed me. I spent time with him and worried about him, and I was okay because then I wouldn't think about—"

Aria. He never says her name. He doesn't have to.

Dad's illness was all Jake had space for, and when he died, there was nothing to help him forget. Nothing but substances that made things fuzzy and made the pain bearable, at least for a while. I didn't know how bad it had gotten until he crashed the truck into a tree, driving home early one morning after a night of partying with a friend.

Finley was a mess. Everyone came home. Mindy drove into town from the city. Taylor cancelled all her plans and drove up to be with them. I merely mentioned the possibility of going home to be with my family, and Ben took my purse and my cell phone and locked me in the bathroom.

I swallow back the lump building in my throat. I don't want to relive that time.

Jake rubs a hand over his head, driving the dark strands into disarray. "We don't use these rooms. We don't talk about our pain. We pretend things are fine when they're not. He wouldn't have wanted this."

"You can always talk to me." I reach out and touch his arm with careful fingers. "I know I wasn't here before, but I'm here now. I promise I'll always be here."

He's probably mad. He should be mad at me. I wasn't here when he needed me most. He should resent me. He and Finley both.

"Why didn't you tell me?" Jake searches my face, his eyes dark and anguished.

Confusion clouds my mind. "What do you mean?"

"I should have noticed something wasn't right with you and Ben." He swallows.

My mouth pops open in surprise. "You weren't responsible for any of that. I got caught up, and I did my best to hide it from everyone. I was ashamed and embarrassed, and Ben did everything he could to cut me off from friends and family. We can blame him."

His hand slashes down in a sharp gesture. "I was too caught up in my own bullshit."

I sigh. "No, *I* was too caught up in my bullshit."

He shakes his head. "It's not your fault."

"That's what my therapist keeps saying, but it doesn't make it any easier to believe."

He huffs a short, humorless laugh. "Yeah. Same."

"We're like two peas in the same shame-spiraling pod."

I can't believe I've been feeling guilty about not being here for him, and he's felt just as guilty for the same reason. We need to talk more, share more. There shouldn't be so much resistance to asking for help. We're family. Maybe this can be our start in moving in the right direction.

I want to pull Jake into my arms and console him, but he's stiff, staring into the dark room, arms folded over his chest.

"Jake, you should know you did help me. When you were in the hospital, I wanted to come home. Ben made me feel like I was being selfish."

I shut my eyes against the memory and the humiliation. It was so obvious for so long, and I didn't see it. Or I saw it and was incapable of changing it, like I had lost control of not only everything around me but myself as well. I still don't understand how or why. It was like I was under a spell.

"You were the impetus that helped me get out. My love and concern for you overpowered my fear of Ben, which was all-consuming."

Jake turns and pulls me into his chest. "I'm glad," he says, his voice rough. "I'm glad that something good came out of something that really sucked."

A short, watery laugh escapes me. I blink away the moisture building in my eyes.

He rubs my back a couple times, speaking so low I have to strain to hear the words. "I feel like I'm walking a tightrope. I think about drinking every day. Sometimes, I'm so close to snapping I can almost taste it. All I want to do is forget what I lost."

I get it. Who wouldn't want to forget the crap our family has endured? The need to escape can be overwhelming at times. I was able to cope by losing myself in my work, and I think Finley and Mindy could say the same, but Jake... he and Aria weren't just siblings. They were twins. And he was with her when she died. I can't imagine. But I also know that Aria wouldn't want him to suffer. I don't know what to say to make it better—nothing can, really, but I have to try.

"If there's anything death has taught me, it's that you need to live. Really live. You never know when it will be over," I say.

I need to take my own advice and stop letting Ben get in the way of me living my life the way I want. I have to stop letting the past dictate my present and future.

Jake releases me. "I don't know if I'm ready to let go."

"It's not about letting go. None of us could ever let Aria go. It's about moving on. Making choices to honor her memory."

His head drops, then he nudges me with his knee. "I guess it's either that or death by cross-stitch."

I laugh, covering my mouth to muffle the sound. "Archer is a good guy."

"I'm glad Finley has him even though I want to punch him in the balls half the time."

We stand there for a few more minutes, talking about nothing important, until I think I might fall asleep on my feet. By the time I make my way back to my bed, I'm spent and exhausted but in a good way. It's like a giant invisible boulder that's been living in my stomach, pressing on my lungs, has suddenly shrunk, and I can breathe again.

Oliver

"Are you sure you've never done this before?"

I shrug. "Not to my recollection."

I've caught four fish, Archer's caught one, and Jacob has caught three bushes and an empty Coke can.

"How is this possible?" Jake retrieves his line from where it's caught under a rock near the shore.

"When the bobber dips, you yank up. It's not rocket science. Children can do it," I say. The act itself is repetitive and dull. I'd rather be cross-stitching—at least I'd be creating something.

Jacob squints at Archer. "Why did you invite him again?"

The air is fresh and clean, the birds are chirping, and a

slight breeze rustles the leaves overhead. *Miserable.* But also, not really.

After fishing and eating a lunch of sandwiches packed in the cooler Archer brought, we move on to axe throwing. It's less boring than fishing but is similarly pointless. Although it gets a lot more interesting when Piper and Finley join us.

"Did you have fun fishing?" Finley asks when they meet us in the grove of trees next to the pond. They've set up thick wooden planks with bright-pink targets spray-painted in the center.

"Oliver did," Jacob grumbles.

Piper stops close enough to me that our arms brush. "Hey."

"Hey." I take in her smiling face, the flush on her cheeks, and the shine in her eyes.

"Oliver, you're up." Archer hands me an axe.

I walk over to where they've marked a spot in the dirt. Eyeing the target, I heft the weight of the axe in my hand for a few seconds. Then I toss it. It hits the *x* in the center of the wooden board.

"You've never done this before, either?" Jake's voice is higher than normal.

I glance at him. "No."

He kicks at the ground with the toe of his boot, shaking his head. "Un-freaking-believable. There has to be something you suck at."

I shrug. "Not that I'm aware of."

Archer chuckles.

We spend the next hour throwing axes at the makeshift

targets and chatting. Well, everyone else chats. I mostly listen and observe. Piper is more relaxed than she has been for the past couple of weeks. She keeps glancing at me and makes a point to stand near me and include me in conversations. I'm not quite sure what to make of it.

For some reason, every time Archer throws an axe, he shares a heated glance with Finley, and the longer we spend, the worse it gets. Eventually, they cut the activity short because they insist we have to go back to the house to freshen up before dinner.

I spend an hour in my cabin alone and a half hour talking to Carson—who still sounds like a robot. Then I futz with the terrible Wi-Fi before I finally give up.

Around five, everyone meets up again at the firepit and outdoor kitchen area set in the center of the camp. We sit on benches around the firepit and eat grilled burgers and hot dogs. Somehow, Piper ends up next to me again, her arm brushing mine occasionally as we all eat. I clean my plate, keeping my focus on the flickering flames in the firepit, letting the easy conversation flow around me.

"Who wants to play cornhole?" Archer asks after dinner.

Jacob stands up from his seat across the fire, wiping his hands on his jeans. "Have you ever played, Oliver?"

My brows rise. "Haven't had the pleasure."

He twirls a finger in a circle. "Great. Someone else play him first."

"We should make s'mores too." Finley looks at Archer.

Archer nods at me. "Oliver, you want to come with me while they're getting the boards?"

"Sure." I make my way to the cart parked nearby.

He brushes a kiss on Finley's lips even though we'll be gone for five minutes max. Then he joins me at the cart and climbs into the driver's side.

He drives, glancing at me in the passenger seat. "Are you having a good time?"

"Sure. Why?" I grab the metal bar near my head as he navigates a bump in the dirt road.

"You seem, I don't know, bored?"

"I'm not bored."

"Good." He turns up the incline drive toward the main house. "So. About you and Piper."

My shoulders tense.

"I see the way you look at her."

"And what way is that?" I keep my voice dry and impersonal.

"Like she's the only thing that makes you feel."

I should have expected this conversation, the one where he scares me away from Piper. She is the delicate princess, and I am the devouring dragon. It makes sense, yet part of me burns at the assumption, anyway.

Archer knows me better than almost anyone. He understands me in a way no one else does. I always feel a little like an exposed nerve around him, like he could wound me without a thought, but the fact that he might begrudge my relationship with Piper is like a knife in the gut.

"I would never hurt her."

He parks the cart and turns in the seat. "I also see the way she looks at you."

My ears prick, all my focus centering in on his words. "How is that?"

He rests his elbow on the steering wheel. "Like she's been walking through the desert for three years and you're an oasis."

I frown in confusion. "Where are you going with this?"

"You're the closest thing I have to family—you and Mason—but Piper is my family now too. Sometimes people get hurt despite having the best intentions."

I press my lips together. The only reason I don't ignore him completely or brush him off with a curt comment is because of our shared history. "I don't think you understand. I would rip out my own heart before I would do anything to hurt her."

Archer nods. "I know. I'm not worried about Piper. I'm worried about you."

An owl hoots in the distance. Leaves rustle in the tree overhead. I stare at Archer, baffled. "Are you very stoned?" *Where's the lecture and the recrimination for wanting to put my foul fingers on Piper?*

"No. I'm dead serious."

"You're worried about my delicate nature?"

He grins. "Actually, yeah, I am. You keep everything inside except for irritation and general superiority. But with Piper, you're different. Sort of. I mean, you're still an ass, but you do things you wouldn't normally. You came here and took time off from working, not because I asked but because Piper wanted to be here."

"And you think she will hurt me and not the other way around?"

"I guess, my concern is that Piper is still healing. Maybe she isn't ready for your level of intensity, and she might spook easy. And yeah, I don't want you to get hurt." With that, he slides out of the seat and heads into the house.

I follow, stewing on his words. *Archer is worried about me?* It's unfathomable.

Inside, he grabs graham crackers and marshmallows from the pantry and hands me a package of chocolate candy bars and another of peanut butter cups. Then we fill a bag with a variety of nonalcoholic drinks from the fridge. My mind is churning, flipping through parts of our conversation like a stack of cards then going back through them, turning them over more slowly, one at a time, considering the impact.

Piper wants me. I know this. She's said as much, but she wants us to be friends. Friends with more. Perhaps she believes that's all she's currently capable of.

With anyone else, I would be fine being a rebound. A strictly benefits guy. But this is Piper. She knocks down all my defensives like they're as thin and ephemeral as butterfly wings.

We load up the back of the cart, and then we're coasting back down the driveway. I try to find the words. "How do I...?" I can't finish the sentence.

I hate asking for help. As long as I can remember, I've taken care of myself. I don't need anyone. I've learned you should never reveal how much you want something. Desire is weakness. Showing your hand is opening yourself up for mockery and dismissal and loss.

I try again. "How do you do it? How do you make it work? How do you let go of everything we went through—everything that made you who you are?"

He shrugs. "I don't. I share it." He looks at me. "Show her some of your dark pieces. Share the things inside you that scare you. Take them out, let her look at them, and see how she reacts." He brings the cart to a stop, parking between the cabin and the firepit.

How can I show her the dark slices of my past and not scare her off?

But they are part of who I am. I can't be anything else.

"You say that like it's easy," I say.

The others are over to the side, playing cornhole, their conversation and laughter audible. Finley says something, and Piper throws back her head and laughs. My chest hurts.

Archer chuckles softly. "It's anything but easy."

"How do you get past the fear?" I ask.

We get out of the cart, and he hands me one of the bags from the back. "Being vulnerable with someone you care for is one of the most frightening experiences in human existence, which means it's also one of the most courageous things you can do."

You have to be brave to be weak. The concept is baffling yet accurate.

Nineteen

Oliver

A few hours later, I'm sitting by the fire alone. Everyone went up to sleep.

We played cornhole. I beat Jake, and then Piper beat me with a last-minute win. I blame the general distraction of her presence.

Even now, the lingering traces of her perfume tickle my senses with the bright, floral notes. I stare at the flames, mulling over the last couple of days. I consider Archer's revelations, Piper's proposition, and the way she watches me like I'm an interesting predator and she doesn't know whether to run or pounce.

Submission is inevitable. Piper Fox was inevitable. From the moment I saw *Lamentation* and had to make it mine, the woman was next. *If she had any idea of the power she holds over me, has always held over me...*

As if conjuring her with my incessant thoughts, I catch the gleam of white clothing moving toward me in the darkness beyond the light of the fire. She stops in front of me, the dancing flames flickering over her skimpy tank top and thin sleep pants. She's like a siren or nymph.

After only a second, she sinks down on the bench seat beside me, inches away. Her hair is pulled back in a messy bun, her face clean and fresh. "Can't sleep?" Her voice is low, husky.

Every conversation I've had with Piper is burned into my memory, especially the one we had the night we slept in each other's arms. I hardly have to think to respond. "No. Hardly ever. You?"

She shakes her head, a smile tugging at her lips. She remembers too. "What time are we leaving in the morning?"

"I have a meeting at eleven thirty, so by eight would be ideal."

"Okay."

The fire pops. I soak in her presence, learning the rhythms of her inhalations and exhalations.

"Are you sure you don't want to stay?" I ask.

She pivots toward me. "What? No. Did you want—you don't want me to drive back with you? Is it because of what I said the other night?"

"No. Not because of that. You seem happier here."

She watches me like she can see into all the dark places I

try to hide. "I love my family, I love being with them, but being home is hard."

"Why?"

She crosses one leg over the other, inclined toward me, her knee an inch from mine. "It reminds me of when Dad died, and the guilt... it's too much."

My fingers ache to touch her, to soothe the hurt in her tone, but the movements aren't familiar to me. "How did he die?"

"Cancer."

I may not be able to comfort, but I can give her something. I clench my fists and open up a vein and bleed. "I never knew my father."

She goes still as stone.

I concentrate on the flickering flames. "He died when I was five. I have vague recollections, just snapshots, really. He liked football. He took me miniature golfing to a place with a giant shoe and a waterfall. He gave me a stuffed raccoon for Christmas when I was four. Then he was gone, and my mother never spoke of him again. I only know his name because it's on my birth certificate."

"She didn't tell you anything about him?" Her voice is gentle as the breeze.

"No. She didn't do well after he died. Then she overdosed when I was eight." The words are flat, delivered without emotion. "She had been sober for a few weeks, maybe a month, before she died. Those few weeks of sobriety were the most normal of my life. I had clean clothes, there was food on the table, and she was there. It was a home. I was too young at the time to truly understand what was going on."

Piper rests against my arm, sharing her warmth and comfort.

"Then she used again, and it killed her. I was at school when it happened, but I heard the adults talking about it while I was waiting for social services in the administration office. It happens a lot, the school counselor said. People relapse and don't realize their tolerance has changed. Overdose is common."

But it felt rather uncommon to me.

I sit motionless, absorbing Piper's care, her touch, taking whatever she's willing to give. After a few long minutes, I break the silence, my curiosity about Piper eating at me. It's probably wrong of me to ask about her life, knowing she'll share anything after what I told her of myself, but I'm incapable of stopping.

"Why does being here make you feel guilty?" I ask.

She shifts even closer, and now the length of her thigh presses against mine. "I wasn't here when dad got sick. We all broke apart after Aria died. I was eighteen. I left. I needed to escape. I became consumed with using my art as an outlet for my grief."

"*Lamentation.*"

She nods. "Yes. Dad got sick shortly after Aria died. I knew he had cancer, I knew Jake and Finley had to take care of him, I knew he was withering away, and still, I stayed away. I came home for the funeral, but it was too late by then. He was gone."

Words are useless in the face of regret. Past situations can't be altered or fixed. There's no use in wallowing in something you can't change. I've rid myself of such useless emotions as regret, but Piper's voice wrenches at places inside of me that have long been dead.

I lift my arm, drape it over Piper's shoulders, and tug her more firmly into my side. She turns into me, one hand clutching at my shirt. We sit there, holding onto each other, until the fire dies and the night deepens.

"I should go." Her hand releases me.

She stands, stretching her limbs. The hem of her tank top rides up a little, exposing a silky strip of skin right above her sleep pants. Cold seeps into me at the spot where she once was even as my body flushes with arousal.

I stand. I don't want her to leave. My mind shuffles through ways I can make her stay. "That night we spent together—I haven't slept that well since."

The corners of her mouth tip up. "Why do you think that is?"

I shake my head slowly. "I don't know." But maybe I do. Something about Piper is safe.

She grins. "I told you the head rubbing would help."

My brows lift at her choice of words, and I almost smile. "And so it did." I drop my voice to a low, heated murmur.

A laugh bursts out of her. "You know that's not what I meant."

Her joy after all that we shared—the darkness she poured out—amazes me. *I made her laugh. Me.* Her delight fills my chest, expanding outward. My face stretches.

Her jaw drops. "Oliver." She steps closer, reaching for my cheek. Her palm slides against my jaw.

Not being touched for a long time does something to a person. It's as if a cold ache settles into your bones. Piper's sweet gesture punches through that cold, sending warmth into the very fiber of my being.

She swallows, her fingers stopping on my cheek. "You haven't shaved."

I let go of restraint, just a little, giving into the urges I've shoved down into the abyss for so long. I tilt my head, leaning it farther into her palm, reveling in her touch. "Is that a problem?"

"No." She takes another step, one palm still resting on my face. Her other arm reaches up. Careful fingers slide through my hair, pulling me down.

I allow it. I can't fight it. My heart picks up a ferocious pace.

Her eyes are heavy lidded, her mouth parted slightly, her chest rising and falling with quickening breaths. Then her lips press against mine. Sensations shudder through me like a thousand-volt shock. Stunned, my body freezes, unable to process her soft mouth, her gentle hands.

And then her tongue flicks out, searching. Primal need surges, breaking through the astonishment. My arms go around her, pulling her closer. My mouth opens, taking control of the kiss. One of my hands moves up her back and cups the back of her neck.

I crave her, my hunger deep and unfathomable. Blood thrums through my veins, making a direct path south. I've wanted her with an all-consuming intensity I've been trying to avoid. And now she's in my arms, all soft heat and fresh-linen scent. I break the kiss to trail my lips across her jaw and down her neck and to flirt with her collarbone.

She sucks in air. Her arms lift, and she pulls down the strap on her tank top, one side then the other. The fabric clings to her curves, not falling but hanging by the merest strand. With one slight breeze, it would fall, exposing her chest. I've never wished more for a gust of wind.

Reining in every shred of self-control in my possession, I draw away, but my hands still clutch at her waist. I want to feel her everywhere. I want to make her insane with need for me so she never leaves. I don't want this to be a one-time deal. I don't want to be a rebound.

One time would never be enough. Even ten times likely wouldn't be enough. The thought is both thrilling and dangerous.

She moves her hands over mine then clutches at my fingers, lifting them up and placing them over her breasts. My pulse goes wild. I can barely breathe.

I flick the fabric down and stare. She's perfectly propor-tioned, her skin pebbling in the cool night air. Everything about her is like a dream. She fits perfectly in my palm. Care-fully, gently, wanting to savor every second, every taste, I dip my head and brush my mouth against her nipple.

She gasps, her fingers weaving into my hair, holding me in place. She doesn't need to worry about me leaving. I'm not going anywhere. I lick her with exquisite care, forcing myself to move with restraint, acting with a tenderness that nearly cripples me. I rub my lips over her breasts, mapping them with brushes of my mouth. I slide one hand lower, my knuckle grazing the thin fabric between her legs.

"Oliver," she moans.

The sound caresses my exposed nerve endings, charging down my spine, feeding my growing arousal. My erection pushes against the zipper of my pants.

Holy hell. This might be over before it begins.

"Let's go inside," she pants.

CHAPTER
Twenty

Excitement coils in my belly, and my skin tingles with anticipation. Oliver moves with catlike quickness, dousing the fire with a bucket of water then grabbing my hand and dragging me into the house and up the stairs. He finally releases me, and I kick off my sandals and perch on the edge of the bed, gripping the comforter with nerveless fingers. I'm breathing hard, my pulse a roar in my ears.

My top is coiled around my waist. I should feel self-conscious—I probably look ridiculous—but how can I think about any of that when Oliver is devouring me with his gaze like I'm the most absorbing thing he's ever seen?

He prowls toward me, a lion stalking its prey. "I want to taste you."

My eyes widen. Heat swamps me. "Yes."

I recline against the comforter as he moves on top of me, placing his arms on either side of my head. Then we're kissing again, except to call it something as simple as kissing is like calling Oliver *a little* rich. He consumes me, his hands roaming my face and hair, his tongue skimming mine. I grapple with the buttons on his shirt while he nips at my lips.

And then he's on the move, slipping downward. He pauses over my breasts, ratcheting up the spiraling tension. I squirm and gasp.

His fingers trip down my stomach, tugging my tank top where it's still looped around my waist. In one brisk motion, all my clothes—including my panties—are stripped down and off my legs, and he's shouldering himself between my thighs. Anticipation swirling in my stomach blends into worry and embarrassment. I haven't been with anyone in a while, and I've never...

I grip his hair, lifting his head up without resistance. "I've never done this." My voice is a little hoarse.

He blinks at me, eyes hazy with lust and need. The words register, and he gives me a feral grin. "Good," he growls and then dips his head again and... *Oh my.*

What if he doesn't like it? What if I don't like it? What if —oh no. When was the last time I shaved?

He kisses my inner thigh, and I gasp. His breath puffs against my skin, and then an eternity later, his mouth is on me, gentle but insistent, and all thoughts fly out of my brain, replaced by nothing but sensation. His lips slide up and down, taking his time, exploring, learning. When he strokes at a certain angle and my thighs clench, he repeats the motion. Testing. Tasting. It's as if he's cataloguing my responses to his every move. Each brush of his mouth pushes me closer to the edge, the pressure gradually increasing until I'm jerking my hips underneath him, begging for more.

He ambushes me with his tongue and his lips, and then his fingers join in pushing me higher and higher until my whole body is a tightly woven knot of pleasure. The tension crests and bursts, and I fall over the cliff, breaking into a million shattered stars.

When my awareness finally knots itself back together, I'm lying on top of a fully clothed Oliver, his heart thudding under my ear. One of his hands is in my hair, sometimes rubbing my scalp, sometimes tugging lightly on the strands, while his other hand grasps my rear in a hold that screams possession.

After a few minutes of assessing our positions, I blink my eyes open. His pants are tented with his arousal. *Why isn't he trying to get me to return the pleasure?*

His lips touch my head. The orgasm, combined with the affection, makes my heart ache not only because this is the first time I've done anything with someone other than Ben—although maybe that's part of it—but also because of how sweet Oliver is. He insisted that he doesn't know how to care, yet here he is, caring.

I lurch into motion, straddling his hips. He stares up at me, his eyes clouded with lust. His hands skim up my arms.

"Piper." His hips move, thrusting his hardness up against me, seeking relief.

Even though I just came, arousal floods through me. Again. I put a hand on his cheek, wanting to feel the stubble on his jaw again.

He turns his head, his lips brushing my palm with a tenderness reserved only for me. His warm hands slide over my back. His gaze locks with mine, heated and somehow adoring. He holds me like I'm precious.

The ice wall inside me cracks open. My entire body stills, my throat closing up. I've been pushing my feelings down, and now all the pent-up shame and anguish is jostling to break through but getting stuck halfway out.

Oliver's voice coming from far away. "Piper? Are you okay?"

I'm not okay, but I can't tell him. My muscles lock. I can't move. Warmth fills my eyes, Oliver's face blurring underneath me.

Oh no. I can't do this. I can't have a meltdown now in front of Oliver, when I'm naked on top of him and we just—

My chest tightens. Black spots crowd my vision. I can't breathe. It's like sucking air through the tiniest of straws.

Then his voice is in my ear, low and soothing, repeating the same phrase over and over. "Breathe with me. Breathe with me."

Time passes. I focus on his voice, on the strength of his arms around me. I'm sitting in his lap, with one of his hands rubbing up and down my back as he continues the calming mantra in my ear.

I take a deeper breath, the thunder in my head easing, my body slowly relaxing. Ben isn't here. I'm here with Oliver, who helped me off the ledge of a complete panic attack.

Oh no. Mortification sweeps in as the panic slinks out.

I cover my face with my hands. "I'm so sorry."

"Please. Don't apologize."

Moving my hands, I force myself to meet his gaze. His concern only makes me feel worse. "But we were…" I swallow. "You were, and I—" I can't even say it. I rub my face.

"You did nothing wrong. Are you okay? Do you want me to walk you back to the main house? Maybe get some water? Tell me what you need."

I stare at him. He means it. He's sincere. He practically vibrates with the need to fuss over me. He's not angry. He's not upset I stopped him when he was so aroused, even though we were clearly moving down the path to the point of no return. Not only that, but I'm sitting in his lap, and there's a blanket wrapped around me, as if he understood that being covered would make me feel less vulnerable.

Ben would have been pissed. Any even slight ding to his confidence—anything he could perceive as rejection—made him angry. And having a panic attack while on top of him would have been registered as rejection. I could never tell him no.

But not Oliver. He's not defensive or pushy in the slightest. He's worried. He's taking care of me yet again, the man who insists he doesn't know how.

I don't want to leave. I don't want to walk back to the

house. Exhaustion weighs me down, seeping into my skin. I want comfort and quiet and him.

"Can I stay here? We don't—I'm not asking you to—"

He rubs my back. "We'll only sleep. I promise."

"Yes. I need to use the bathroom."

He lifts me like I weigh nothing, sets me on my feet, and then bends over to pick up my pajamas. He hands them to me.

I clasp the bundle against my chest and whisper, "Thank you," before escaping into the bathroom.

When I return from the bathroom, Oliver is in bed. He left the light on my side on, and he's set a glass of water next to it. I click off the lamp, slide under the covers, and lie there, staring at the ceiling.

"Do you need anything?" His voice is quiet in the darkness.

In response, I shift closer, rolling so that my back is flushed right up against him. He turns and spoons me, his arm over my waist, his legs tucked up behind mine. His chest is bare, and the skin-to-skin contact relaxes me. I'm surrounded. Safe.

Within minutes, I'm asleep.

———

I'm so warm and comfortable I don't want to wake up. The warmth shifts behind me, and awareness slithers through my limbs and shoots sparks to my slumbering thoughts.

I'm wrapped in Oliver, his arm around my waist, our legs

tangled, his nose close enough to the back of my neck that every breath he takes is a rhythmic brush against my skin. He smells like cedar and soap and clean linens.

When he smiled last night... it was a revelation. He went from merely handsome to devastating. I've seen his lips soften and quirk, and I've seen amusement light his eyes, but the sight of a true smile destroyed all my willpower.

It was addictive, his happiness. I had to touch him. I had to taste him.

And apparently, he had to taste me. Heat suffuses me. Memories shuffle through my mind—his warms hands on me, his usually severe mouth turning gentle against my skin. The way he kissed me like he needed me to breathe... the way he brought me pleasure, and when I froze and panicked, he stopped even though he was not yet sated. He helped me and held me, and it was enough. Then we slept curled around each other like we'd been lovers for a decade.

The arousal that swamps me is overwhelming. It was never like this with Ben, not even in the beginning. It's almost too much. I could quickly become addicted. My feelings for Oliver are so strong that he could break me apart. I'm both terrified and exhilarated.

He moves, and something soft brushes my skin, right where my neck meets my shoulder.

Did he kiss me? I shiver.

More. I arch my back, pressing against him, the hardness of his erection a brand against my lower back.

Heat coalesces in my stomach.

He sucks in a sharp breath. "Piper." My name is a hoarsely whispered prayer. His arm tightens around me.

"Oliver. Touch me. It's okay. I'm okay. I want this. I want you."

He kisses the side of my neck, nipping tenderly. His morning stubble scratches my skin, shooting a frisson of pleasure down my spine.

I have to see him. I twist my head around, wanting to add a memory of Oliver all drowsy with sleep, unshaven and disheveled. It's like a secret, and I'm the only one who knows.

My breath catches in my lungs as I devour the sight. I run my hand along his jaw. The stubble highlights the harsh edges of his face, yet he's somehow softer this way—less severe, more real.

His free hand skates up my side, covers my breast, and gently toys with me through the thin layer of cotton, and all my thoughts flee like birds startled out of a bush. My heart pounds in my ears, impossibly loud. The thumping seems to be in surround sound, echoing through my body and banging on the front door.

Wait. Front door?

"Hey, Oliver, you awake? Finley made breakfa—oh God!" Over the banister separating the loft from the living area below, Jake's face comes into view, twisted into an expression of pure horror.

He bolts back outside, the door slamming shut behind him.

I roll over and hide my face into Oliver's chest, embarrassed laughter breaking out of me.

"Are you okay?" he asks, his hand rubbing circles on my back.

I pull back and look at him. His eyes are dark with concern.

"I'm fine. I just had to be the one facing the door so he got a good view of you feeling me up." I laugh again, harder, ducking my head into him.

His chest shakes underneath my cheek, and I lift my gaze. He's smiling. No. It's more. He's laughing.

I blink at him. It's a rusty, almost noiseless laugh, hardly even a chuckle, but it's there, and it's true.

"I've never heard you laugh." I rest the tips of my fingers against the soft skin of his mouth.

The curve in his lips falters, dipping slightly. I remove my hand and then sweep my mouth across his, a quick, involuntary movement. His fingers brush my cheek, his eyes searching mine, and his expression defaults to its normal serious mien.

"We should probably go up for breakfast. We need to get on the road," I say.

"Right." He watches me, his eyes dark and hot. His hair is askew, and stubble shades his jaw.

I don't want to move. I want to take in this rumpled version of Oliver for at least a few more hours.

He releases me, rolls away, and spins to a sitting position on the edge of the bed, his back facing me—and what a back it is, corded with smooth muscles.

His hands clench the comforter. "If you keep looking at me like that, we'll never leave this loft."

I press my lips together, holding in my laughter. "How do you know I'm looking?"

"I can feel it." His back muscles tense.

I bite my lip to contain the groan wanting to erupt. "So you're threatening me with a good time?"

He twists around, reaching for me.

With a laugh I skitter away and head for the stairs. "Later!" I call.

CHAPTER
Twenty~One

There's no way I'm going to sneak back up into my room in my pajamas without everyone seeing me. I trudge up the path, breathing in the damp early morning air. The temperature is quiet and cool, not yet flush with the heat of the day, as I make my way around the bend of the driveway and come across Jake.

"How could this happen again? I knocked this time," he grumbles to himself, pacing back and forth.

"Hey, Jake."

He stops and faces me, shoving his hands in his pockets.

"I, um, sorry?" I grimace.

I'm not sorry about Oliver's hands on me, the brush of his lips, the care in his touch. I can't regret it. I do regret my brother witnessing his older sister getting fondled.

"It's fine. It happens." He sighs and then mutters, "To some more than others."

"What does that mean?"

He rubs the back of his neck. "Nothing I want to talk about. So. You and Oliver, huh?"

I take a few steps closer to him. "Yeah."

"Is it serious?"

I cross my arms. "I don't know yet." It feels serious. It feels like everything. I bite my lip. "I wanted to find out if he really is good at everything he does."

Jake groans, covering his face with his hands. "I know you didn't just make a sex joke."

I crack up.

He just shakes his head and then squints at me for a few seconds. "You want to get back in the house without running into Archer and Finley?"

"Yes, please."

He nods, spinning on his heel. "I'll go around and unlock the front door. They're in the kitchen, so you can sneak up the stairs."

Relieved, I follow. I make it upstairs without being spotted, change into my traveling clothes for the trip back, and head back down like I've been there all night. Oliver is sitting at the table, plunging a serving spoon into a heap of scrambled eggs.

Our eyes lock, and a thread of panic slithers through me. *What if he changes his mind?*

But then the harsh line of his mouth softens.

I hold back a grin.

"Are you gonna actually eat any of those eggs, or are you just trying to seduce them?" Jake asks.

Oliver dumps the eggs onto his plate and hands the bowl to Jake, our moment of silent communication broken. I take my seat next to Oliver.

"Sleep good, Piper?" Finley asks, grabbing a slice of toast off another plate.

"Yeah, Piper, how *did* you sleep?" Jake asks, his tone sarcastic enough that Finley shoots him a sharp look.

"Great, thanks. Will you pass the bacon?"

Archer passes me the plate.

I take a second to stare down at the bacon before shooting Jake a devilish smirk. "Too bad. I was really hoping for sausage."

He chokes on his orange juice.

Archer claps him on the back. "You're not supposed to breathe it."

Once we're done eating, Oliver and I grab our bags and the box of tractor pieces to load up the car.

"Drive safe. Tell Mindy to call me." Finley squeezes my shoulders.

Oliver and Jake shake hands, and then Archer gives Oliver a manly back pat that's almost a hug, but not quite. Finley hugs Oliver, who stands there like a human statue, his arms stiff at his sides. The scene shouldn't be so cute. It makes me smile.

Oliver insists on driving home since I drove us here.

"Don't you have work to do?"

His regard skims over me. "I'm not sure I could concentrate."

I flush with heat.

Once we're on the road, I understand the concentration comment more. I can't stop staring at him. The familiar trees and hills outside the window are not diverting enough to pull my attention away from the man behind the wheel. He's in one of his standard impeccably fitted three-piece suits, a navy blue one. He still hasn't shaved, and the stubble along his jawline is distracting. I've never seen it in broad daylight. He looks like a businessman-slash-pirate.

Shiver me timbers, indeed.

"You didn't shave," I say.

"You seemed to like it this morning." His voice is steady and low. He rubs his jaw, and the side of his neck flushes red.

I press my lips together to contain the grin threatening to spread across my face. To distract myself from his presence, I text Mindy that we're on our way home, but she doesn't respond. *Hm. Weird. Well, she's got to be at work now, so she's probably too busy to reply.* I suspect Mindy has had a certain married, allegedly separated musician keeping her busy this weekend, because she never answered my texts.

I relax back in the seat and give in to the urge to watch Oliver drive, his hands on the wheel confident and sure, his focus absolute—like it always is. My mind flips through scenes from the prior evening, before my embarrassing meltdown. It amazes me that Oliver has risen so far to become who he is.

I want to know what happened after his parents died, how he went from orphan to successful businessman, but the warm interior of the car, combined with the soothing hum of the tires, pushes me into a sleepy state. I doze in the sunshine that forces its way through the tinted windows of the SUV.

The next thing I know, I'm blinking at the front of Mindy's building. I rub my eyes. "Oh. We're here. Sorry, I fell asleep. Worst copilot ever."

"You needed the rest." His voice is low and intimate.

I smile at him. "Thank you for—"

"Who is that?" His eyes focus behind me.

I follow his gaze to the front stoop. There's a man peering into the door glass. He wears a baseball cap pulled low, and sunglasses cover half his face. He's holding a paper bag and two cups of coffee.

"I think that's Blake Bonham. He works with Mindy." I frown. It's almost noon on a Monday, and he looks like he just rolled out of bed. *Is Mindy not working today?* "He's probably waiting for her. Maybe they had a meeting or something."

I am the worst liar. I would love to tell Oliver about what's going on, but I can't break Mindy's trust.

Fortunately, he changes the subject. "Have dinner with me."

"Yes." My response is immediate.

One corner of his mouth tilts up in the smallest of curves. "Tonight."

I nod. "I have work to do, so I'll be downstairs in a couple hours."

My stomach ripples with anxiety. I have the work space. I have the tools and the pieces from Whitby, along with all the other recycled parts Oliver got for me at my demand. I have an idea. No more excuses—I need to make something. Multiple somethings. I have a little over two months, and who knows how many hours it will take to assemble the final products.

"After you're done working, come upstairs. Six okay?"

"Okay." I lean over and kiss him. I intended for it to be a quick goodbye kiss, but the second our lips touch, it's impossible to pull away. I get lost for a long minute, enjoying the feel of him.

His teeth nip at me before he draws back. "Let me help you bring your bag upstairs."

I grin against his mouth. "You'll be late for your meeting."

His tongue flicks against my smile. "Fuck my meeting."

"I'll bring an overnight bag tonight."

His eyes search mine, full of naked heat, a fire in their depths. "Are you sure?"

"I'm sure." One corner of my mouth curves up. "It's the only way I'll get any sleep." Although my thoughts aren't really preoccupied with the sleeping part of our arrangement.

A smile creases his face, taking my breath away again. I give him one last kiss and a cheeky grin. Then I'm out of the car, slinging my bag over my shoulder.

I walk up to the porch. "Hey, Blake."

He lifts a disposable cup at me in a semblance of a wave. "Mindy is upstairs, still sleeping. We had a late night. I snuck out to get coffee and didn't grab a key or my cell phone." He chuckles. "I was trying to be sweet and got myself locked out."

I step around him to the door, key in hand. "I hope you weren't stuck out here too long."

He shakes his head. "Only a few minutes."

I unlock the door and then turn to him. "Here, let me help you carry something."

I reach for the cup in his hand with the bag, but at the same time he pushes the other cup toward me. There's a bit of uncomfortable fumbling, and I drop my keys. I bend over to pick them up while he holds the door with a foot. Laughing and awkward, we somehow manage to get inside.

"Did you have a nice weekend?" he asks.

"Yeah, it was great."

I don't know what else to say. I can hardly ask how his weekend was since we both know he spent it alone with Mindy in her apartment and they had the whole place to themselves and probably had so much wild monkey sex she's not going into work for the first time in her life. I really don't want to think about it.

The rest of the quiet elevator ride is worse than our clumsy scene on the porch. I have no idea what you're supposed to say to your sister's married lover. Once we're back in the apartment, he disappears into Mindy's bedroom with the coffees, and I make my way to the guest room. I need to shower and get ready for the day, not to mention pack a bag for tonight.

Eager excitement curls through me. I can't wait to see

Oliver again, even though I spent the entire weekend with him and literally just left his presence. In my room, I fling my bag down on the full-size bed and go to grab fresh clothes. A package on the antique oak dresser stops me in my tracks.

The printed label is addressed to me, and there's no return address. My stomach sinks. *Why would Mindy put this in here? She has to know who it's from.*

Maybe I'm wrong. Maybe it was delivered by a client or a fan or my new business manager. Grabbing a pen, I hack through the tape enough to open the box and pull out a lacy light-pink piece of lingerie. *Ugh. Gross.*

A folded piece of paper rests at the bottom. I pick it up and read: *For you and your new boyfriend.*

Unease traces its ice-cold finger up my spine, my body flashing with the chill of apprehension. My phone chimes, and the tendrils of alarm expand into a fist of dread. It's a text from an unknown number: *Do you like your present? You could put it on right now, and I'll come upstairs to see it.*

My stomach churning, I race over to my window and nudge aside the curtain to peer down at the street. A couple walks down the sidewalk hand in hand. A jogger runs in the opposite direction, her blond ponytail bobbing. A white sedan cruises down the street.

He's not here. He's just messing with me. He wants me to be afraid.

I can't let him win.

Twenty-Two

OLIVER

I glance at the clock for the thirtieth time in as many minutes. It's nearly six. Stirring the simmering sauce on the stove, I force myself to take a deep breath, hold it, and then let it out slowly. Anticipation riots in my pulse, and nerves buzz in my chest.

It's been a long time since I've cooked, though my current effort is hardly difficult since I had my chef prep all the necessary ingredients. Once I could afford someone to cook all my meals, I delegated the task. It was what made the most sense, saving me time, but it was also a symbol, a stepping stone to propel me that much farther from my past, moving me beyond a time when I was a feral child who had to scavenge for meals.

I ram those memories into a box that's shoved into a dark

corner of my mind. I can't think of that now. Tonight has to be perfect.

I tug at the sleeve of my shirt. I'm not used to being dressed casually unless I'm going to sleep or something. My suit has become like a uniform, but more than that, it's like armor or a costume. It's what I put on to remind myself of who I've become and who I will never be again.

I found my current outfit tucked into a drawer in the recesses of my closet: jeans and a dark long-sleeved Henley, thin and soft. She wanted me in jeans. I hope she likes it.

I check the clock again. A minute hasn't even gone by since I last looked. Sighing, I pick up my phone and scroll through emails to distract myself.

I archive a few messages from Carson that outline issues with a property deal. He briefed me before he left today. His work was impeccable as always, but his normal enthusiasm was muted, and then he left early. He never leaves early.

The phone rings, vibrating in my hand. Brienne. I told the staff to keep me apprised of Piper's movements while she worked today in her studio. I answer immediately.

"Miss Fox is on her way up in the elevator."

"Thank you. That should be all for the night. Please make sure there are no interruptions," I say.

"Yes, sir."

The urge to stand by the elevator doors, tapping a foot in impatience is nearly overwhelming, but I manage to restrain myself, staying at the stove, stirring the sauce so it doesn't burn.

The elevator dings, and I call, "In here!"

There's a pause, and then her heels click in the tiled entry, the beat echoing in time with my accelerating pulse. Her gaze behind me is a palpable brush on the side of my face.

"It smells amazing," she says.

I turn. She's wearing a dress, a bright, frilly thing, all whites and yellows in a floral pattern. The hem flirts with her knees. A black bag, larger than a purse but smaller than a backpack, is slung over her shoulder.

"You look—" Words fail me. She's utterly perfect.

She approaches me slowly, as if I might spook, stopping for a second to slide the bag from her shoulder and set it on the counter. When she reaches me, her eyes dip down my frame and then take their time back up. "You look as good as I thought you would in jeans."

I stare at her. She means it.

She grins at me. "I dressed up, and you dressed down."

I still can't speak. Her smile dips a little. I feel like I'm being rude, but I can't help it. I'm too amazed that she's here. That she came. That she wore a dress for me. I want to touch her again so badly it's almost painful.

She steps closer, her perfume tickling my nose. "Will that keep for a bit?" She tilts her head toward the stove.

I reach over, turn the burner down to the lowest setting, and then find my voice. "The longer it simmers, the better the flavors are. Did you need to do something before dinner?"

Her hands run up my forearms, sliding along the fabric. They slow down over my biceps and squeeze a little before settling on my shoulders. Tingles rush through me every-where she touches.

What is she doing? Whatever it is, I don't want her to stop.

"There is something I need to do." Her voice is hushed. Her hands draw me closer and closer. "Something very important." And then her mouth is on mine. Soft, sweet, insistent, and overwhelming.

My mind, normally racing at a thousand miles a second, jumping from one to-do item to another, goes opaque. Only one thought consumes every fiber of my being: Piper.

Her lips. Her tongue brushing mine. Her hands moving from my shoulders to my neck. Her scent filling my lungs. The smoothness of her dress when I run my hands down her spine.

She leaps without warning, and I catch her under her thighs, lifting her just as she wraps her legs around me. Without conscious thought, I carry her into the living room, still kissing, and lay her on the couch on her back. Her dress rides up between us as I settle my hips between her thighs, holding myself up to lick at her mouth.

She arches, rubbing herself against my straining erection. Blood rushes in my ears. I grapple with the quickly unrav-eling threads of my self-control.

I kiss down her neck and run my lips against her collar-bone and my finger plays with the strap of her dress before trailing lower. "Is this okay?"

"Yes. Please."

Holding myself up with one arm, I use the other hand to

carefully, slip the strap off her shoulder, tugging the top of the dress down. *Sweet Jesus.* She's not wearing a bra. My breath stutters to a halt in my lungs.

Her hands skate up my arms to cup my face. I focus on her eyes. She smiles. Her head turns, and she brushes a kiss against my forearm where the rigid limb is supporting my weight.

The affectionate movement nearly breaks me in two. The world shudders to halt, my vision going black.

"Are you okay?" Her thumb strokes my cheek.

"I..." Every time she touches me like I mean something to her, it's as if I've been ripped apart and then pieced back together. *How can I ever be the same?*

My phone rings. I blink down at her, the real world rushing back in. Dragging myself off Piper, I pull my phone out of my pocket and sit on the couch.

It's Brienne. It must be an emergency. She knows what *no interruptions* means.

"I have to take this," I tell Piper. "Brienne." I put the phone to my ear.

Piper sits up next to me, straightening her dress.

"Carson is here, sir, and he's, uh, unwell. He is insistent on speaking with you. I've told him you're otherwise occupied, but he's—" There's a crash and a thud on the other line. "Will someone pick him up?" she calls out.

"Brienne."

"Yes, sir?"

"Speak plainly."

"He's drunk. And crying. A lot. And he just tried to throw himself into the trash can."

I take in Piper—the concern in her eyes, her cheeks still flushed with desire, her lips pink and swollen. I swallow back the curse words threatening to erupt. My eyes fall shut.

"Send him up." I end the call and chuck the phone onto the coffee table before leaning over and wrapping my arms around Piper's waist, dropping my forehead onto her shoulder, taking a second to inhale.

"Is everything okay?" She lifts a hand to my shoulder, and the other rubs my neck in light, soothing motions.

"Carson is here. He's on his way up and apparently inebriated. I knew something was wrong with him." I draw back.

Her expression is troubled. "I hope he's okay."

Me too. "We'll see in a second."

Through extreme force of will, I remove my hands from Piper and push to standing, taking a deep breath before heading to the elevator. Piper follows, her tread light behind me. I glance at her. The shoes are gone—on the floor somewhere probably. She's adjusting her clothes, smoothing her hair. I like her like this, shoeless and slightly mussed.

"You look beautiful." I tug her into me and give her a quick, hard kiss before turning my attention to the man stumbling out of the elevator.

Carson's pink tie is tugged loose and his cuffs unbuttoned. His hair sticks up like he's been running rough fingers through the usually perfect coiffure. His eyes are red rimmed and bleary.

"I'm sorry, sir. I didn't want to bother you, but I didn't know where else to go." He slumps against the wall.

Piper rushes over to him and touches his arm. "Were you robbed?"

He waves a clumsy hand. "No. Nothing like that."

Piper jerks her head toward the living room, her brows raised. "Why don't you go sit down in the living room with Oliver while I make some coffee?"

I stare at her for a few seconds. There was a nonverbal cue in there somewhere. She wants me to talk to Carson while she makes herself scarce. Right. I am totally not going to screw this up.

I sigh and take Carson's arm. "Come on." I half drag him into the living room. "Let's sit down."

In the living room, I drop Carson into the leather loveseat, and I sit on the couch. I told him he could come to me with whatever he needed, but I didn't think he would actually do it. Carson, like me, is a workaholic who keeps his personal life separate from his professional life, except he does it with a lot more flair and animation.

"Do you want to tell me what's going on?" I ask in the tone one might use requesting a lobotomy.

"James and I broke up." He covers his face with his hands. "I had to run home before CrossFit. I forgot my gym clothes—that's why I left early. I went home, and James was in our room, getting fit with someone else."

His words are slurred, his tone bitter. I have no idea how to respond.

"I walked in and saw"—one hand leaves his face and

makes a circling motion—"what I saw, and then I left. Like a chump. I didn't say anything. I don't even know if they noticed I was there."

Piper walks in and hands Carson a mug. He takes it in shaking hands and then regards it bleakly. She sits on the sofa next to me, close enough that our thighs touch. An electrical zing of energy throbs from the spot.

Now is not the time. I focus on Carson.

Still gazing sightlessly into the coffee, he continues. "We've been together for five years. How could he do this? I don't understand what's happening." His voice cracks.

I share a glance with Piper. *Now what do we do?*

"Lambda Lounge," Carson says suddenly, his voice overly loud.

We stare at him.

"That's where we met. That's where I was, just now, and where I..." His lashes flutter, then he jerks up. His eyes meet mine, flick to Piper, and then back to me. They widen. "I'm drunk." He stands. The cup in his hands tilts, precariously close to sloshing out all over my carpet. "I'm drunk, and I'm here. And you're here." He gestures to Piper, the mug tipping again. "What am I doing here?"

I stand and take the cup from him before he ruins my Isfahan rug. "It's fine. Sit."

He drops back into the loveseat.

I hand him the mug once he's no longer a danger to my belongings. "Drink."

He sips, his brows lifted.

I take the cup away again, just in case. Then I sit next to Piper.

"Do you have anyone we could call?" Piper asks gently.

"No. My family is in Georgia." His gaze shifts to me. "I could rent one of the staff apartments..."

"They're occupied."

His body droops, sinking farther into the loveseat.

"You can stay here." The words are out before I can consider them too closely. "I have a spare room and bath on the north side of the building." My own rooms are on the south. I could comfortably house an entire family or three and not even notice.

Carson stares at me. "I couldn't."

"It's fine." I almost barking the words.

He flinches.

I sigh and stand up. "Come on. I'll show you. You may want to get some rest. You're going to be terribly embarrassed in the morning, and I'm never going to let you forget it."

Twenty-Three

PIPER

Oliver shoots me a deer-in-the-headlights look over Carson's shoulder, so I follow them down the hall on the other side of the kitchen to what apparently is the north wing of the building. I thought the custom-tiled open entry, state-of-the-art kitchen, and wall of windows facing Central Park were impressive, but it isn't until we're hoofing down various hallways, passing door after door, that I realize how considerable Oliver's domain is. Most of the doors are closed, but a few are ajar just enough for me to peek in and catch a glimpse of a home gym, a small movie theater, and an office with wall-to-wall bookshelves.

Holy crap. A library. Finley was right—it is like Beauty and the Beast. *Does that make Carson Mrs. Potts? Nah, he's definitely Lumiere.*

We finally stop in a luxurious guest room that's bigger than Mindy's entire apartment and looks like something straight out of an HGTV show. There's an attached bathroom with a Jacuzzi tub and a glass shower, all lined with blue mosaic tiles that match the comforter on the king-size bed. Carson sinks down on a plush chair in a sitting area in the corner, holding his head in his hands.

Oliver frowns down at him. "Do you need pain reliever?"

"I need a Mark reliever," he groans.

Mark must be his boyfriend. I know the sentiment.

"I'll stay with him if you want to grab him some essentials." I touch Oliver's arm. "Maybe some water too?"

His hand covers mine, and he nods. "I'll be right back. There's a smaller kitchen on this side of the building, and it's stocked, so I won't be long."

I sit in the chair across from Carson. *Another kitchen. How many kitchens does a billionaire need?*

After a minute of silence, Carson removes his hands from his face. "Piper," he says like he's just now realizing I'm here.

"Do you need anything?"

"I have to tell you something."

"Okay."

He leans forward so far I lift my hands in preparation in case he falls on his face. "His birthday is Thursday," he says in a stage whisper as if he's imparting an imperial secret.

"Oliver's birthday?"

"Nobody knows. I only found out because he got an email from his dentist."

"Does he have any plans?" I ask.

He wrinkles his nose. "What do you think? No. He doesn't do anything but work. Last weekend was the first time he's unplugged for more than a couple hours for as long as I've known him. He might not even remember it's his own birthday." He reaches out, his hand grabbing mine. "I'm glad he has you."

I pat the hand covering mine. "I'm glad he has you too."

He releases me with a sigh, slumping in the seat, his head falling back, his eyes shutting. "He thinks he stole me from Guy, but Guy encouraged me to take the job. He said Oliver needed me, but now I wonder if he realized I would need him." He snorts out a little laugh, and then his breathing evens out, and within seconds, he's snoring.

I smile. It's kind of adorable. But then my thoughts turn back to Oliver. His birthday is in a couple of days. I wonder if Archer knows. I'll have to call Finley tomorrow and check. He never would have said anything. I never would have known if Carson hadn't shown up here, drunk and sad. *Poor Carson.*

Oliver returns, a bag in his arms. He takes in Carson snoring in the chair, rolls his eyes, sets the bag on the ground, and then bends over and hauls Carson up. Dipping under his shoulder, he carts him over to the bed. He tugs off Carson's shoes and gets him under the covers, still completely dressed and still snoring.

I rummage through the bag on the floor. Oliver brought a half dozen water bottles, a ream of crackers, a bottle of pain reliever, and... a giant candy bar. *Is he worried Carson's going to be hungover or pregnant?*

I hold it up, my focus narrowing at the writing on the wrapper. "Is this imported?"

One shoulder lifts. "It's his favorite." He stalks over, grabs the bag, and sets the items on the nightstand in neat, orderly rows.

He just happens to have Carson's favorite imported chocolate in his apartment. My heart swells. This man is so much more than he even realizes. He tucks his employee into bed, fussing like a mother hen.

Once that's all done, and Carson is still snoring despite being jerked around like a giant drunk doll, we head back through the maze of hallways. I have to bite my lip to hold in the goofy grin threatening to spread over my face.

"Are you hungry?" he asks.

He's walking in front of me and therefore can't see me ogling his butt in his jeans when I answer. "Starved."

He must hear something in my voice because he stops and turns to face me. I take one more step. We're close enough to touch.

His gaze is a hot touch caressing my skin. "Do you still want to stay?"

"Yes."

"We don't have to—you don't have to do anything you aren't comfortable with. I would never—" He shakes his head. "I would never presume."

He never stutters or stumbles. I suppress a smile, lifting a hand and resting it on his cheek. He still hasn't shaved. Dark scruff contours his jaw.

"I know. That's why I want to stay," I say.

His hand covers mine on his cheek. He swallows, his eyes searching mine. We move at the same time, a frenzy of motion, touching, seeking, tasting.

"I want you," he says against my lips.

I smile, remembering when I spoke those same words to him. "Bedroom," I murmur.

"Yes." With one hard kiss, he releases me and grabs my hand, and then we're running.

Well, he's running, and I'm tripping and laughing behind him, clutching at his fingers as he speeds around corners and back through the kitchen and then through a labyrinth of corridors into his bedroom.

He flicks on the light. There's no time to examine his personal space as, without warning, his mouth covers mine, consuming me with bone-meltingly deep strokes of his tongue.

I fumble at his clothes, yanking at his shirt.

I haven't had my chance to explore him. I want to taste him like he's tasted me and then run my hands up and down the smooth muscles of his back, lick every inch of his sinewy body, and drive him as crazy as he makes me feel. I break the kiss to rip his shirt over his head. He tosses it aside, and then we both pull my dress up and off, and it joins his shirt somewhere on the floor. He tugs at the button of his jeans, his fingers trembling.

I cover his hands with mine. "Let me."

Sinking to my knees, I undo the button then lower the zipper slowly and carefully over the straining bulge. His breathing is ragged, his hands fisting at his sides. I peer up at him. His pupils are blown, his lips parted.

"You can touch me," I say.

After a second's hesitation, his hands weave into my hair, soft and seeking. I pull his boxer briefs down, and his erection springs out. Tasting him isn't a choice—it's a necessity. My mouth covers him, licking, sucking, breathing in his tart scent, like soap and heat and man. He groans, long and loud, his hands tightening against my scalp. I want to be the one who shatters his unrelenting control.

"Piper." My name on his lips is a benediction. "I can't . . ."

Fisting the base, I suck harder. In a whirlwind of movement, he jerks out of my grasp, steps out of his clothes, and hauls me into his arms, taking us to the bed.

"I haven't nearly spent enough time playing," I say.

"Later." He forces the word out as he tumbles backward onto the comforter, keeping me on top of him and shifting our weight so I straddle his hips, his erection sliding against my wet heat.

It feels so good I throw my head back and thrust against him over and over, his rigid length stroking all the right spots. His hands come up and cup my breasts, thumbing my nipples, and I almost fall apart right then. I want him inside me now. No more waiting. No more interruptions. He's right. Playing can come later.

His hands skim over me, gripping my hips in place even

as I shift to take him inside me. "Condom," he says through gritted teeth.

"Where?" I pant.

"Side table."

It only takes a second. I rip the package open with my teeth and slide it on him, his breathing growing more ragged with my touch. And then I'm straddling him again. I lift up and sink down on top of him.

CHAPTER
Twenty~Four

OLIVER

Piper is heaven around me. It's unbearable. I can't last. I can't come yet. I have to make this good for her.

She whimpers. I home in on her face. Her expression is dreamy, eyes hot and drowsy.

Our gazes lock and hold. She moves on top of me, slowly rising and falling. I soak in the warmth of her body and the tenderness in her touch, taking it into my being, where it fills up all the dark, cold places.

Her smile is a comet streaking across the sky, making my heart twinge. She leans over, her lips seeking mine as she moves, taking me with erotic abandon. The needy sounds tumbling out of her mouth enflame my body, shoving my desire into the stratosphere.

I'm going to combust. Burst into flames. Grabbing at her hips, I thrust up into her, curving my body to reach with my mouth wherever I can taste her skin. I can't be slow and soft —not now.

She meets my frenetic pace, her hands gripping my shoulders. My mind blanks, and my body locks, my spine arching as I surrender and plunge into the depths of pleasure, barely registering when Piper falls over the cliff right behind me.

When the haze of postcoital bliss lifts around the edges, Piper is sprawled over my chest, her finger trailing patterns against my skin. I'm holding her against me, my fingers cupping the curve of her ass. It's my hand's favorite new resting place. I'm more relaxed than I've been in years. Or ever. I don't think I've ever felt this boneless and peaceful.

She lifts her head. "Do you think dinner is ruined?"

I move her hair back with a finger. "Are you hungry?"

"Pretty sure I've worked up an appetite." Her cheeks tint with pink.

"We can't have that. You'll need more energy."

Because once was not enough, especially with us being as hurried and frantic as we were. I need more time with Piper, to explore and play and discover everything she likes, everything that makes her squirm and release those breathy little noises. This will never be a rebound. It will never be temporary or casual. *Casual* is anathema to every thought I have about Piper.

"Stay here. I'll get it." With one final squeeze of her rear, I roll out from underneath her.

She snuggles into the bed, her eyes following me as I stalk across the room to grab a pair of cotton shorts from the walk-in closet.

I return, bending over to brush a kiss against her lips. "I'll be right back."

She smacks my ass as I turn away. "Hurry."

Fighting the smile tugging at my lips—I've never smiled so much in my life—I make it to the kitchen in record time. The sauce is a little burned, but I can't even muster up the energy to care. With Piper, I don't have to be perfect—I can just be.

I mix the sauce and pasta, grab extra snacks and waters, and haul all of it to the bedroom. Piper is lying in bed on her side, still naked, uncovered, and completely uninhibited. Desire courses through me, all my blood heading to the center of my body.

She eyes my growing arousal and then tosses me a sultry smile. I try not to stumble over my feet and drop the food everywhere. I barely manage to get it perched onto the table at the foot of the bed.

Then I pounce on her. Her laugh is sultry and resonant, and I feel it deep in my chest when I cover her body and capture her mouth with mine. Food no longer my primary concern, I settle between her legs.

Wait. Condom. I reach over the bed, rooting for the box of condoms.

"Oliver."

I stop fumbling and look down at her.

She bites her lip. "I'm on the pill, and I'm clean. I was tested after... after, even though we always used protection. Are you, do you—"

I swallow, my pulse thudding. "I'm clean." I search her face. "I've never been with anyone else without a condom. And as I mentioned, it's been... a while."

Her fingers grip my shoulders. "Are you sure?"

I nod. "Are you?"

"Yes." Her whole body relaxes, and she winds her limbs around me.

I pull my mouth from hers, and keeping our gazes locked, I slide against her slick heat, slipping up and down. Her breath falters. Her mouth parts, her chest rising and falling.

Jesus Christ, how have I lived without this? Without her?

I notch the head of my cock at her entrance and push in, just an inch, then pull out. She whimpers, her pupils dilating, her hips shifting under me, seeking more. I repeat the movement, gliding in halfway then moving back.

"Oliver," she groans.

Without warning, I thrust in to the hilt. She gasps.

"Is this okay?" I ask.

"God, yes." She stirs under me, her hips lifting, encouraging me to move. "You feel so good."

I fight the urge to pound into her over and over. Not this time. Leisurely, I pull out and then drive back in, keeping my gaze on hers, making the movements steady.

She stares right back, her eyes hazy with desire. Her

fingers rub against my neck and trail down my back. I take her slowly, deliberately, over and over.

Every thrust is achingly sweet. Every touch is raw. Every glance is tender. I angle my hips and monitor her every reaction, learning how she likes it, seeking the position that will shove her into pleasure. When she finally escapes into bliss, I follow, letting go of all the rigid control tying me together and surrendering every piece of myself into her waiting arms.

———

"Will you tell me how you met Archer?" Her voice is easy, light, and undemanding.

I'm aware that I don't have to answer, and I know she won't press or push or be upset if I choose to keep my secrets to myself. Maybe it's because she understands, or maybe it's because of the safe cocoon of her arms around me or the darkness enveloping both of us in a soft embrace, but I want to tell her. I'm not afraid to share the dark pieces of my past. I know with bone-deep certainty that she has the compassion and the strength to carry them with me.

I stroke her arm, reveling in her softness. "After my mom died, I went to live with my aunt. My mother's aunt, actually. She was kind to me, but she was in her seventies. She died when I was ten, and there was no one else, so I went into the system."

She lifts her head slightly and rests her chin on my chest, her hair tickling my skin.

"It wasn't all bad," I tell her, reading the fear in her eyes. The assurances won't last long. This isn't a fairy tale. "Most of the families I was placed with were well intentioned, if overwhelmed. But I didn't stay in those homes for long." Sighing, I pick up a strand of her hair and rub it between my fingers. "An unshakable fact about humanity is that some people are kind and doing their best, and others, when given any little grain of power, become tyrants."

I'm self-aware enough to acknowledge that this is where the crux of my relationship issues began. I lost both of my parents at a young age, then I lost my aunt, and then I lived with monsters. It doesn't take a psychotherapist to recognize my abandonment issues and the emotional detachment I've relied on to survive.

A crease appears between her brows, and I stroke it with my thumb.

"I ended up with a couple who had a half a dozen other fosters. I was a damaged child. I got in fights, snuck out, broke every rule they tried to impose. They didn't do anything that would leave a mark. They couldn't afford to lose any of us since they were paid per child, and the more care a child required, the more they received. But they used every type of nonphysical punishment possible to assert their control. They would lock me in a small dark closet for days. Withhold food. Threaten to harm the others if I didn't obey."

Her hands tighten on my chest.

"I finally realized the only way I could win, the only way

I could truly be free, was to take action. Running away and living on the streets wasn't an option. That's where troubled kids are lured away by true monsters. I needed a better plan. I was always good in school without even trying, so I focused my attention on improving my grades enough to get scholarships. Then I applied for the youth summer camp without telling my foster parents. They couldn't fight it without drawing attention. It was an escape even if only temporary."

Piper is tense in my arms, but her gaze is soft.

"Archer and I were placed in the same cabin. We weren't friends, not at first. I was angry at the world, ready to fight everyone who looked at me the wrong way. That's when I started hoarding food."

I don't feel shame over the act, not anymore. I recognize that I was only a child trying to survive, but the memories are still sharp and jagged.

"I would hide it under my bunk, in my bags. I saved what I could stuff in my pockets during mealtimes, but then I also snuck into the kitchens at night and stole. It was a compulsion. Having a stockpile gave me control. It made me feel safe." I swallow. "When you live in chaos as a child, you'll do anything to impose order on the world."

Her lips brush my chest then move up and graze my jaw, a sweet comfort.

Some of my tension falls away. I keep going. "One night, when I snuck out and broke into the kitchen, there was a group of other boys in there, waiting. They jumped me."

Her eyes widen.

I wave a dismissive hand. "It wasn't the first time. They

had messed with me before. I was small for my age, and bullies love an easy target. But Archer had heard me sneaking out and followed. He helped me fight them off. And you've seen him—he's the size of a small mountain. He's always big. After that, the boys left me alone, and Archer and I formed an alliance."

"And then you met Mason after that?"

I nod. Mason lives in LA. Piper met him when she left Ben. She had nowhere to go and reached out to Finley for help. Archer called Mason, since he was in the area, and Mason got to Piper first and took her somewhere safe to wait while we flew out to get her.

"What about Guy?" she asks.

"We met in high school. I had applied for a scholarship to a prep school and started there my junior year. There was student housing, so I no longer needed to live in foster care."

"And so you escaped." She scoots up my chest and kisses my mouth with soft lips, resting her nose against mine. "Thank you for trusting me with your story. You're amazing, Oliver. Strong and resilient. You did what you had to do to survive."

I bask in her gaze, her words, her body pressed against me, her accepting nature. She understands. Of course she does. Our scars are not the same, yet they mirror each other all the same.

I lift my head the barest inch to bring our mouths together again. Our lips graze, seeking affection and comfort, our hands moving over each other in soothing strokes. This isn't an embrace of desire but one of reassurance and relief. It goes on and on. I could touch Piper forever.

"You are a survivor as well," I tell her, brushing her hair back when we eventually break apart.

"Yes." Then her eyes widen. "I forgot to tell you—I got another package from Ben."

Twenty-Five

Piper

His body goes rigid with tension. He sits up on his elbows. "When?"

"It was on my dresser when I got home. I'm not sure when it came in. I didn't see Mindy before I left to come here, so I couldn't ask."

"What was it?" His eyes are full of concern.

I grimace. "Lingerie."

His face turns into thunder.

"There was a typed note with it. He knows about us somehow."

His brows furrow. "What did the note say exactly?"

"It said, 'for you and your new boyfriend.' How ick is that? And how does he know about us?"

His jaw hardens. "I don't know, but I intend to find out."

Frustration sinks into me. Not at Oliver—at Ben. And at myself for ever choosing him. "I hate that he's still affecting my life."

Oliver strokes my back with long brushes of his fingertips. "It won't be forever. We'll take care of it. You're not alone in this."

"I still worry." I swallow. "Even with you, I worry that I'm going to do something wrong, say the wrong thing, and it will make you angry."

"You're safe with me." His voice is low and serious, and his face has that intense focus, concentrated on me. "That doesn't mean I won't get upset sometimes. I'm human. But my emotions aren't your responsibility—they're mine. I want you to be honest with me, and I'll be honest with you."

He has no idea what his words mean to me. "Ben held me responsible for everything. Well, all the bad things. He took credit for anything good."

His jaw hardens into steel.

"I was always on pins and needles, walking on eggshells all the time." I search for the words, wanting him to understand. "It was like walking through the same minefield every day, but they constantly moved. Some days, a random comment wouldn't bother him in the slightest, but the next day, that same phrase would set him off. It was impossible to predict."

"He was a weak fool."

"I was the fool," I say. Oliver opens his mouth to contradict me, and I cover his lips with gentle fingers. "When I met Ben, I was grappling with so much guilt. So much shame. When Dad died, everything was overwhelming. Ben was charismatic, handsome, so seemingly perfect. When things started going bad, deep inside I thought it was no more than I deserved. How could I be allowed joy when my little sister was dead? When my father got sick, and I couldn't even visit? I was a mess. Ben was a monster, but I wasn't perfect, either. My pain was like a knife, and it cut him too."

He cups my face in his warm hands, smoothing his thumbs over my cheeks. When he speaks, his voice is rough with emotion. "You never need to soften your edges for a man who doesn't have a sharp enough tool."

I'm struck speechless. He's right. What I'm going through now is like grief, but it's not the loss of Ben that I'm mourning—it's the loss of myself. The lack of trust in my intuition. I've lost part of my innocence, my youthful hopes and expectations.

I have to forgive myself, relearn how to have faith in my internal compass. *How do you hang on to hope when it can lead to more hurt?*

And I need to be honest with Oliver. He still doesn't know I haven't even started working on the pieces I promised him. I have to trust him with my fears, with all of my scars, like he trusted me.

My thoughts grow cloudy with fatigue. All the sharing—and the mind-blowing sex—has exhausted my mind and body. Wrapped in Oliver's arms, drained and completely sated, I slide into a dreamless sleep.

———

I wake up in darkness, still wrapped up in Oliver. His breathing is deep and steady. Still sleeping. Memories of the night before flicker to life in my mind's eye, and warmth fills me.

My muscles ache in the best of ways, and just thinking about him sends heat flooding to those achy areas. I'm tempted to wake him with my mouth, fall back into pleasure, but... I know how precious sleep is for him.

Besides, my mind is churning, my fingers tingling with a familiar itching. I think I know what I need to do. An image is forming in my mind. I need to create.

Carefully, I extricate myself from Oliver's heavy limbs and make my silent way out of his room and into the kitchen, where my bag is still sitting on the counter. Fortunately, I don't run into anyone while I'm sneaking around in the dark, naked. Once I have my jeans and T-shirt on, I jot down a quick note and leave it on the counter.

Then I take the elevator down to the garage and into the space Oliver made just for me. My insides get all melty thinking about it. That was him, taking care of me even then, back when his voice was cold and his features impassive.

I go back to the drawing table, where I was working yesterday, and rip the notebook to the next clean sheet. The pencil moves across the table and… it's not terrible. My shoulders slump.

Finally. I know the result won't be exactly what's on the page. The piece will change shape and melt and mold into something different—that's how it always works. But I know, with an artist's intuition, that this is it. This is where I need to start. The beginning of anything is always terrifying and exhilarating.

Twenty-Six

Oliver

I wake up, alone and immediately alert. *Was last night a fever dream?*

No. My sheets still smell like Piper's perfume. And sex. A lot of sex.

Despite the anxiety pinching my nerves with the familiar terror of loss and abandonment, I'm more relaxed than I've ever been in my life. I quickly assess the room for evidence of Piper. Her clothes are still scattered around the floor along with my own, but there's no sign of the woman herself.

I heave myself out of bed, throw on the cotton shorts from last night, and head to the kitchen to see if her bag is still here. It's gone, but there's a note where it used to sit. I snatch it up.

Went downstairs to work XOXO - P

The urge to run downstairs and spend my morning with her is nearly overpowering, even if it's just watching her work. *No. Pull it together, man.*

I am more than willing to rearrange my entire schedule—hell, my entire life—around her. Being with her last night—the way she touched me, the way she listened and shared—was like being taken apart piece by piece and then reassembled into something new and singular. I could never let anyone else have that much control over me. But with Piper, it's always been a slippery slope, and even more horrifying, I find that I don't mind it.

I'm ready to hand her my beating, bloody, brutalized heart and ask nicely for her to please not crush it between her delicate palms. *Perplexing. And yet not.*

Forcing my limbs to obey my commands, I return to my bedroom, shove myself into workout clothes, and go into the gym. The familiar movements and the drumming of my feet on the treadmill pound my thoughts into a more organized pattern. While I'm running, I call Arnold and give him some of the details about the package Piper received from Ben.

"I haven't seen Mr. Simon since the party in Brooklyn," Arnold says.

But Arnold has been keeping an eye outside Piper's apartment only during the daylight hours. I've been more worried about her safety than about Ben's precise whereabouts, as long as he was nowhere near her.

"I want eyes on her apartment twenty-four seven. If that means bringing in additional staff, I'll cover it. If you see him, call me immediately."

"Got it," he says.

We disconnect. I increase the speed on the treadmill, my mind conjuring the details of everything Piper has told me about Ben, about how he treated her. Anger is a creature with claws and teeth, and it wants to rip his head off. Even though I know she's downstairs and perfectly safe, part of me frets, and the lingering temptation to go downstairs pummels me with every breath.

I shake my head as if it will shake out the thoughts. Work. I need to get to work. I can't think about what Piper is doing or what she's thinking or if she's going to stay the night again or if she's happy or hungry or confused.

What if she changes her mind? What if everything I shared registers, and she decides all my baggage isn't worth it? What if this is still just a fling, a rebound for her to move on from her ex and onto someone else? I haven't been so unsure of myself since I was a child.

After I finish working out, I shower and get dressed and take the elevator downstairs to my office, scrolling through emails as I walk. The elevator doors slide open. Across the hall, a delivery man in a dark-brown shirt opens the door to the stairwell and he heads down, his hat tugged low and his back to me. The set of his shoulders strikes a familiar chord. A twinge of alarm pings in the back of my mind.

"Mr. Nichols." Carson is standing at the end of the hall, waiting for me, holding a colorful vase.

"What is this?" I stop in front of him.

"Cake pops. They were just delivered." He motions toward where the delivery guy disappeared down the stairs.

He's procured a clean suit and is as pressed and polished as ever. If it weren't for the dark circles clutching at his eyes, I wouldn't know this was the same man I had to carry into bed last night. "You want these?" He lifts the vase slightly.

"No."

He turns and heads back to his desk. "I sent the summary of today's schedule to your calendar."

I follow him. Before I have a chance to so much as open my mouth, he speaks again.

"I, uh..." He puts the cake bouquet down on the edge of his desk and scrubs a hand through his hair. "I would like to apologize both for my behavior last night and for intruding on your evening with Miss Fox."

"No need."

Carson has never been one to simper or prostrate himself before me. I hope this doesn't become a habit.

"I can book myself a hotel room and be out of your guest quarters immediately."

I frown at him. "What about your things?"

He blinks. "My things?"

"Yes, your possessions. You have items you own in your prior apartment, do you not?"

"Well, yes, but—"

"There is no need to sustain the expense of a commercial establishment, especially when you wouldn't have anywhere to store any of your personal belongings. I have plenty of room and storage space."

He stares at me, stricken. I reassess my words, trying to

find the flaw, trying to think through what would have put that expression on his face. *I suppose...*

"If living on my floor makes you uncomfortable, I will pay for a room somewhere, since I offer all employees accommodations, and it's not your fault the current dwellings are otherwise occupied."

He shakes his head. "I don't want to impose on you."

Oh, for heaven's sake. "You'd have your own kitchen, elevator, and stairwell. Don't be ridiculous."

"Oh, my own private stairwell." His voice is dryer than the Sahara. "How can I refuse?"

I scowl at him.

He sighs. "I'll take it. Thank you, Oliver." His voice is low and thick with indecipherable emotion.

Enough of this. I stalk into my office and try to focus on work. At nine, as per my normal routine, breakfast arrives on a tray placed on the table in the sitting area. I move out from my desk and sit to eat.

Has Piper had breakfast? Is she still here?

I call Brienne. "Is Miss Fox still here?"

"Yes, sir."

"Has she eaten?"

"I don't know. I haven't had time to examine the contents of her stomach, sir."

Everyone's a comedian today.

The smile is apparent in her voice when she continues. "She hasn't left the studio since she came down here around five thirty this morning."

I press my lips together, thinking. I don't want to bother

Piper if she's working, but I can't stop trying to take care of her, either.

Brienne continues, oblivious to my inner monologue. "We can let her know there's food upstairs and she can join you if she wishes."

I release a slow breath. "That would be fine. Thank you."

We hang up. *What does Piper like to eat for breakfast?* I stand up and pace.

"Carson," I bark, and he's at the door in a blink. "Have David bring more food."

"What kind of food?"

I shrug. "I don't know. Just... another serving of my usual is fine. And a smoothie. Maybe a doughnut."

His head cocks, a smile threatening at the corners of his mouth. "We have doughnuts?"

"Figure it out," I snap.

Now I can't eat. *What if she doesn't come up? Maybe she's not hungry. Maybe she's busy. And if she does come up here to eat with me, how am I supposed to behave?*

I pace some more. This is ridiculous. We ate together last night... oh, wait. We didn't eat last night. I brought the food in and then got distracted by her naked body.

Good lord, she must be starving. I'm practically torturing her.

I sit down and force myself to take a bite of avocado toast. She's either coming, or she's not, and either way—

A knock at the door makes me jerk my head up. Piper walks in. She's here in jeans and a baggy T-shirt, with her hair pulled back in a braid.

"Hi." She tucks a stray tendril behind one ear.

"Are you hungry?" I gesture to my food.

"Starving. I've been working all morning." She shuts the door behind her, bounces over, and sits in my lap, her body folding against mine like it belongs there. Piper steals the toast from my nerveless fingers and takes a big bite before handing it back and then snuggling farther into me. "What else we got here?"

I can't speak. A mixture of shock and elation fills me to the brim, overflowing my senses. She touches me like it's normal. Like it's easy.

She twists to see my face and then flushes. "Oh. I'm so sorry. I shouldn't have commandeered your food and your... body."

The muscles in her legs tense like she's about to stand. I drop my toast on the table and tug her back. I pull her closer so she can feel exactly how pleased I am to have her in my lap.

"Oh. *Oh*." She wiggles against me.

I groan.

She laughs. I capture the sound with my mouth. And then I completely forget about breakfast and everything else for over an hour.

PIPER

"It was Blake," Mindy says, handing me a glass of red wine before plopping down on the couch beside me.

"How did that happen? Where did he find it?" I take a small sip.

"He said it was sitting outside our front door. I gave him a key on Saturday when I got stuck at work and he was going to get here before I did. It was addressed to you, so he didn't really think about it, just stuck it on your dresser and then forgot." She runs a hand through her hair.

Well, the mystery of how Ben's creepy package made it to my room has been solved. I didn't notify the authorities until today. I've spent the last two days working my fingers to the bone and the last two nights being soothed into sleep by

Oliver-derived orgasms. Not a bad way to cure insomnia. The work is moving along slowly but surely. And the orgasms are as mind-boggling as ever.

I didn't want to come back to Mindy's, but I needed a change of clothes, and Oliver and I have gotten so close, so fast. The urge to move in with him and never leave is strong enough to freak me out. I can't be drawn into something so serious so quickly. I need to keep a piece of myself separate. I can't repeat what happened with Ben. I know Oliver isn't Ben, but the fear still lingers. Oliver is like a hurricane—it would be so easy to be consumed by him.

I have to remember my goals—rebound and get back to work. Although Oliver doesn't feel like a rebound. Not at all. I also wanted to spend some time with Mindy. I haven't seen her since the day we left for Whitby.

I'm not sure I will have four structures done in time for the gallery opening, but I know I'll get one completed, for sure, and I have Oliver to thank for it. He did help me get my mojo back, more than he could possibly understand.

"Is Blake coming over tonight?" I ask Mindy.

She tucks her feet up under her. "No. We had a little argument yesterday."

"What happened?"

She makes a face. "There were pictures in *Page Seven* of him and Jeanette having a romantic dinner."

"Ouch."

She takes a big gulp of wine. "I know it's for show, but that doesn't make it easier to swallow."

"Of course."

She rests her head back on the couch and shuts her eyes. "Only a couple more months, and they will break up, and it will all be good."

"What about your job?"

She waves a hand. "I don't think it will be an issue. They'll have to move me from Blake's account, so I won't work on anything directly related to him or Vacation Mustache. We're both adults. We'll keep it as private as possible, and it will be fine."

I swirl my wineglass. I wouldn't think someone so willing to play the press with his current wife could just step out of it, but what do I know? I hope she's right.

"What about you? Not staying with Oliver tonight?" she asks.

"No. We have plans tomorrow, though, so you'll have the apartment to yourself tomorrow night." I convinced Oliver to take the day off, but I didn't tell him what for. He has no idea that I know it's his birthday. Heck, he may not even realize it's his birthday.

"Are you sure you aren't rushing into things so soon after Ben?"

I take another sip of wine. Even though Mindy is just verbalizing my own inner turmoil, my defensiveness rises to the surface. "It's been over four months now. Besides, Ben and I were over long before that. I just needed the strength to leave."

She bites her lip. "I don't want you to end up in another bad situation."

The irony here isn't lost on me. Mindy isn't exactly

getting herself into a great situation.

"I haven't been attracted to a man in years. Ben made me feel like shit that had been stuck on garbage and thrown into a gutter in the Bronx. Oliver makes me feel... like I'm worth something." *He makes me feel like I'm everything.*

"*You* have to make you feel those ways."

I nod. "I know. He's helped me a lot, though. He's helped me remember who I am."

She snorts. "By being a total ass?"

I smack her leg. "He's not. I mean, he can be, but not to me. You have to get to know him. He has a soft gooey center."

"If you say so. Just promise me you won't get too sucked in. Make sure he doesn't try to cut you off from the rest of us. Let's have a date Friday night. Only us. No men. Dinner and a movie or something."

I grin at her. "Deal."

———

Anticipation bubbles in my veins while Brienne and I wait for Oliver to meet us in the car.

"He's on his way down." Brienne hangs up the phone, her eyes meeting mine in the rearview mirror.

"Thank you." I peer through the tinted glass in the back seat, watching the elevator doors.

I wanted to do something more extravagant for Oliver's birthday, but I had to come up with a plan on fairly short notice. I considered inviting other people—Guy and Scarlett or Finley and Archer—but it was too last-minute. Besides, I wasn't sure if Oliver would appreciate that much attention without fair warning. I'll have to save that for his next birthday.

If we're still together a year from now. We haven't had the whole talk about whether we are exclusively dating each other, but it sure feels like we're pretty damn serious.

I hope he enjoys what I have planned. He has no idea where we're going. I just told him I wanted to spend time with him, and he was all-in. Of course, I made sure he wore something appropriate for the occasion because a three-piece suit will definitely not work.

The car door pops open, and Oliver slides into the seat next to me, his hands going immediately into my hair, tilting my head. "I missed you," he murmurs, and then his mouth claims mine.

Distantly, the window between us and the front seat hums closed, and the car purrs to life underneath us. I lose myself his possessive touch and the carnal sensuality of his mouth, the scent of his cologne wrapping around me.

"I missed you too," I say against his lips when we finally pull back for air. I draw back farther to take him in. "Shorts." I check him out, my gaze dipping over him. "Shorts and a T-shirt."

His lips twist. "As commanded." His voice is dry.

"I like it."

His gaze zeros in on my mouth. "I like it if you like it." He reaches for me again, but the car rolls to a stop.

"We're here!" I grin at him, excitement and nerves making me jittery.

He frowns. "Already? We didn't go very far."

"Come on." I push him out of the car and onto the sidewalk.

Brienne opens the trunk. "Call me when you're ready."

"Thanks, Brienne." I reach into the trunk, grab the water guns, and hand one to Oliver.

He blinks down at the giant orange-and-yellow plastic item in his hands. "What is this?"

"A Super Soaker."

He frowns.

I squeeze the trigger lightly, and a stream of water shoots out of my gun, splashing his shoulder. His brows lift, his mouth popping open in shock. I throw my head back and laugh.

"Oh, you'll pay for that." His voice is dark, liquid heat.

"Not if you don't catch me." I take off running toward the park.

I had Brienne drop us off on Eighty-Sixth Street so we would be as close to the Great Lawn as possible. I dash down a path that cuts through the trees, darting around pedestrians, Oliver hot on my heels. Water soaks my shorts. He's shot me in the right butt cheek.

"Hey." I shoot a laughing glance behind me.

"Just marking my favorite bits."

Delight is a glow in my chest. Cracking up, I almost trip, and Oliver is there before I fall, grasping my elbow. I catch my footing and then keep running.

He keeps pace. He isn't even winded. He could probably catch me without exerting himself in the slightest, but he doesn't. He stays behind me, probably viewing his handiwork on my cotton shorts.

We break out onto the wide expanse of grass that is the Great Lawn, right into the largest water fight in the city.

CHAPTER
Twenty~Eight

Oliver

"What is this?" I stare out over a sea of people, all of them running, laughing, and chasing while jets of water stream in haphazard directions.

Piper is jumping on her toes, all excitement and energy. "It's a water fight. Let's go!"

She runs into the melee, shooting at people erratically, and I follow. I have a feeling I would follow her anywhere, into any battle. I keep my eyes on her back as she runs into the crowd.

Within seconds, we're both soaked. Her wet clothes cling to her skin, and her hair is damp against the nape of her neck. Minutes later, we stop near the center of the massive crowd.

She faces me, tilting her head back, shutting her eyes, and spreading her arms out while water rains down on us.

Rivulets flow down her face and onto her black tank top, an astute choice of color. My own white T-shirt is molded to my body, concealing nothing.

She laughs into the sky, her eyes shut. She's stunning. Heart-stopping. Her bliss is like the most potent drug flooding my veins, filling my chest with unequivocal joy.

Without warning, she reaches for me, twists my wet shirt in her hand, and drags me against her. Then we're kissing. Her mouth is hot, but her skin is wet and cool, the contrast an extraordinary assault on the senses.

I drop my gun and haul her closer, aligning our bodies. She melts against me, and the drizzly carnage around us disappears. All that exists is her mouth on mine, her fingers clutching me to her, and her taste—like sunshine and spring breezes.

Eons later, she pulls back. "Happy birthday," she says against my mouth. And then she kisses me again, her lips stealing the astonished gasp from my lungs.

How did she know? Did she plan this for me? I haven't celebrated a birthday in... I don't even know how long it's been.

Then she pushes me away, shoots me in the chest with an animated laugh, and runs off. I chase after her. If I wasn't already completely gone for her, this would have shoved me over the edge.

I've never had so much fun in my life. But it's not the activity—it's her. It's like Piper knows exactly what I need when I couldn't have articulated it myself. She knew that I needed to *play*. I never would have considered involving myself in anything like this.

An hour later, we've abandoned the battle. I'm completely drenched from head to toe, my shoes squelching with every step. She doesn't seem to mind the almost sheer fabric clinging to my body. Her gaze returns to my chest every few seconds as we make our way back to the car.

Brienne is parked off West Drive, waiting for us. Piper grabs the stack of towels, and I haul the cooler up onto my shoulder. Then Piper leads me over to a grassy sunlit area, where she lays out a blanket and hands me one of the towels.

I scrub it against my head, and then fall back on the blanket, closing my eyes against the midday sun. We don't speak. We don't have to. Words are unnecessary.

Piper lies beside me, a comforting presence. I reach for her and weave my fingers through hers. We hold hands and lie in the sunshine for so long that I doze off. Unbelievable.

I rouse when her hand extricates itself from mine, her weight shifting next to me. Rolling onto my side, I prop my head up on my elbow and blink in the vivid light. She's pulling items out of the cooler, setting them down between us.

Two chocolate cupcakes. Plastic cups she fills with fizzing gold liquid—champagne maybe.

I pick up one of the cupcakes. "Scarlett's?"

She sits in front of me, cross-legged, peeling the wrapper off her own little cake. "Yep. It's the one that calls Guy a douchenugget or whatever. I can't remember the full title." She takes a big bite and moans. "Damn, that's good."

I push myself up, lean forward, and kiss her. "Tastes better this way."

She laughs, pushing me away. "I will not feed you like a baby bird."

I swipe some frosting with my finger. "I can think of other ways we could consume these."

Her cheeks tint pink, her eyes going hooded. "I've got more. That sounds like something we could consider later tonight."

"I can't wait."

Twenty-Nine

Piper

Mindy and I are in the middle of retail therapy when she gets a call.

"Are you serious? I told you I needed the night off." Mindy waves an exasperated hand. "I'm at Columbus Circle."

We're walking through the mall, weaving through shoppers, carrying bags of clothes and accoutrements from Williams-Sonoma.

"I'm sorry," she mouths to me.

I wave her off. "It's fine."

She speaks back into her cell. "Ugh. I'll be there as soon as I can." Then she hangs up and looks at me. "I'm sorry. This shouldn't take more than an hour."

"It's fine. I'll meet you back at home. I'll order takeout, and we can watch *The Tenth Kingdom*."

She laughs. "You kids and that show. Come on, we can share a cab part of the way."

I get back to the apartment within the hour, deposit Mindy's bags in her room, and then plop down on the couch so I can text Oliver. I saw him this morning, but already...

I pull him up on my phone and type, *I miss you.* I delete it. Too needy.

But true. I type it out again and then hit Send before I can chicken out.

I toss my phone onto the side table so I won't be tempted to sit there, staring at it like a moonstruck teenager, and then I force myself off the couch and put away the clothes I bought on our shopping spree, including a cute little black number I got for Oliver. I'm walking out of the guest room when a text comes through. I go back and grab my phone, eager.

It's not Oliver. It's Mindy: *I forgot my key.*

I grin and key in, *The great and powerful Fox forgetting something?*

Her reply is almost instantaneous: *Hardy har. I have the one for the building, just not the apartment.*

I type, *It's fine. I'm here to let you in.*

A few minutes pass, and then my phone dings again; *On my way back now.*

Perfect timing. I call the Chinese place down the street to order dinner. I hang up, and almost immediately, my phone dings.

Oliver. It's a picture of him and Carson on his couch, doing cross-stitch. Oliver is grimacing, Carson's wearing a tired smile.

I laugh and type, *Cute.* I tap Send.

A second later I get another text: *I miss you too.*

The grin that spreads my face feels decidedly goofy.

My phone dings again: *Tomorrow?*

It's amazing how he can pack so much into one word.

I type, *I'll be there. Dinner?*

On me, he responds.

I bite my lip, thinking, then send another text: *I bought you a present.*

His reply is almost instant: *It's not my birthday anymore.*

It's sort of for both of us, I reply.

A few seconds later, his response comes through: *Intriguing.*

I laugh.

There's a gentle knock, and I jump up. It's got to be Mindy. The takeout place would have buzzed. I swing open the door. "That was qui—"

Ben.

"How did you get up here?" Shock and trepidation coil inside of me, my muscles locking, my throat squeezing.

He's thinner than he was when I last saw him, skin stretched tight over his face. His jeans are dirty, and a brown T-shirt hangs on his frame. The panic nearly overwhelms me. I can't think straight.

Remember Oliver's calming voice last weekend, I take a

deep breath and exhale slowly. I shouldn't be asking questions. I need to get rid of Ben. Now.

I go to slam the door in his face, and he stops it with one rigid arm thrust out, palm flat on the wood.

I stare at him. "Leave, or I'm calling the cops."

"I haven't seen you in months. I'm in town on business. I was thinking about moving to this area since work is going so well for me and thought I'd stop by and say hi. Don't you want to see me?"

Ben moving to New York? He can't be serious. I don't dignify his question with a response. "What do you want?"

"I have something you need." He winks, the move as smarmy as the way his voice dips with innuendo.

Ugh. How did I ever find him attractive? He's disgusting.

My hand clenches on the doorknob. "I really doubt that."

"Trust me. You want this. If I give this video to the press, you'll be ruined, you and your little boy toy. Or should I say boy toys?"

What the hell is he talking about?

I need to call the cops. My phone is over on the table. I try to work out how I can get to it and how I can get rid of him, but all I can think about is running. Hiding. "You have nothing. I've never done anything to be ruined."

He sneers. "Haven't you?"

My stomach twists, my heart pounding. My words emerge through clenched teeth. I don't want him to hear my voice tremble. "I don't know what you're talking about."

I try to think straight through the mound of terror

smothering me, but it's impossible. Did he take some sort of sex tape or do something while we were together that I'm not aware of? I wouldn't put it past him. It would have been easy to do with his cell phone, which was always in reach.

"What do you want?"

He smiles as if this is what he's been waiting for all along —me asking him to give him whatever he wants and needs. "I just want us to work together again. That's it. I helped make you who you are. You wouldn't be anyone without me. It's not asking for much, don't you think?"

I don't know whether to laugh or cry. Is he serious? Of course he is. He thinks he's the sole reason I achieved any success, like I hadn't made a name for myself in my own right.

I want to scream. I should scream. That would at least get the neighbors to come out.

He takes a step back. "You need me. I made you, and I can break you. You have twenty-four hours to think about it."

With my heart still thumping a mad rhythm, I shut the door and lock it then slide to the floor and try to catch my breath. Adrenaline rushes out of me, leaving me lightheaded. My mind runs through the conversation.

What the hell was he talking about? What is he going to do next?

A knock on the door behind me makes me jump, a wonky scream startling out of me. I spin around and peer through the peephole. *Please be Mindy.* I will never ever open a door again without checking first.

I don't recognize the person on the other side. He's in his thirties, with dark hair cut high and tight. He's stocky with a thick neck.

Maybe it's one of the neighbors coming over to check on me. I don't think Ben and I were loud when we argued, but the whole conversation feels like it happened to someone else.

"What do you want?" I call through the door. My voice is tremulous, shaky.

"Are you okay?"

Maybe it is a neighbor.

"Who are you?" I ask.

"Mr. Nichols asked me to check on you."

"What?" The words don't register. *Oliver? How did he…?*

This doesn't make sense. It's a trick maybe. This guy could be working for Ben.

"Are you okay?" the stranger asks again.

My phone rings. I walk into the living room and pick it up.

"Piper?" It's Oliver. His voice is deep and gruff. "Are you okay?"

Nothing makes sense right now. "What is going on? Who is the man at my door? He said you sent him?"

He hesitates.

"Oliver?"

"He's a bodyguard. I hired him to watch over you."

Thirty

Oliver

She hangs up on me.

My heart stops. *No.*

I call her back. She doesn't answer. I call Arnold.

"Is she okay?"

"I don't think she's bleeding, if that's what you mean, but she might be in shock. She seemed confused and extremely angry."

"Please stay nearby in case Ben returns."

"You got it." He hangs up.

I call her again. Dread is a lead weight in my belly.

She answers and immediately speaks. "You should have told me. When did you hire him? How long has he been following me?"

I wince. "Piper, I—"

"When? When did you hire him?" Her voice is a knife.

"After you told me about the first package from Ben."

There's a long pause. Her voice is soft when she asks, "That long ago?"

I say nothing. I can't defend myself.

Her breathing falters. "That's the real reason you came to the party in Brooklyn. You knew he was there."

"I never lied to you."

"A lie by omission is still a lie."

The words are a blow. But she's right. I've been so used to doing what I want, never considering other people's feelings, until now. Her feelings are the only ones that matter, and I ruined it. I need to fix this.

"I had to do something. I don't trust Ben."

"You don't have to trust Ben—you have to trust me. I told you not once, but twice that I didn't want security and I needed to have control over my own life, and you said you understood. But you didn't, did you?"

I broke her trust. I've always known I don't deserve her. I just thought I would have a little more time with her.

"Ben was staying too close to Mindy's. I was worried about you. I had to keep you safe."

When she speaks again, her voice is low and shaking. "How did you know where he was staying? Why didn't you tell me? Wait," she says before I can answer. "I know exactly why. If you told me, you would have to explain how you've been interfering in my life and making choices for me when you know what I've been through."

My stomach churns, revolting at the thought that she

would think I'm anything like *him*. I'm bleeding inside, and I've never been good at bleeding alone.

"You've been hiding things too," I say.

She pauses. "What?"

"You told me you needed a work space to finish, when the truth was you hadn't even started."

"I was scared."

"Of me?" The words hurt, a physical, throbbing ache in my gut.

"We signed a contract. You take those very seriously."

"Fuck the contract, Piper." My voice lashes.

She gasps. The pain in my core builds. She's just come face-to-face with her abuser. She must be shaken and hurting, and I'm not helping.

I lower my voice. "You have no idea how many contracts I would break for you. This isn't just about me. You don't trust me, either."

She doesn't deny it. I don't know what else to say or do. I want to argue my finer points, convince her to take me as I am, make her promise not to leave me. I want to beg and plead and get on my knees... but this is Piper. I can't treat her like a business deal—like something to be won. I want her to choose me without coercion. But I've always known I'm not the lovable type.

"I'm sorry," I say.

"I know." She sniffs. "I'm sorry too."

"Where does this leave us?"

"I don't know. I need a little time to think."

"Right. Time."

If she needs time, I'll give it to her. I'll rip out my heart and leave it at her feet if she wants it. Although that organ is suspiciously silent.

With nothing left to say, I hang up.

———

"Would you pass those crab things?"

I reach over, grab the container of food from the side table, and pass it to Carson.

"Thanks. Why didn't I know you had a freaking movie theater in here?"

"Because this is probably the first time he's used it," Guy says, shoveling noodles into his mouth with chopsticks.

He's not wrong. We're sitting on the black leather recliners, some ridiculous movie playing on the screen in front of us. I'm not sure what it's about. I stopped paying attention after the credits. Carson insisted it would make me feel better, but all I feel is worthless, wretched, and annoyed.

On screen, the blond woman shoves gourmet chocolates into her mouth.

"Oh, do we have chocolate?" Carson asks.

Guy perks up. "I brought cupcakes."

My whole body recoils. "No cupcakes." My voice is a whip.

Carson smacks my arm with the back of his hand. "Maybe I want cupcakes. You're not the only one going through heartbreak here, you prima donna."

Guy laughs.

I scowl. "So glad we're amusing you."

I can't tell them why I'm so averse to cupcakes, especially Scarlett's cupcakes, which is probably the type that Guy brought with him. It doesn't matter. It's not the cupcakes' fault. Everything reminds me of Piper. My office, my bed, my car... water. I can't even hydrate without thinking about her.

She's still been using the studio space downstairs, but we haven't talked, texted, or seen each other at all over the past four days, three hours, and—I check my watch—twenty-seven minutes. Carson said the three of us needed breakup bonding time, and as a sign of my mental destabilization, I didn't even question it. I immediately called Guy and then ordered mass quantities of food. I let Carson pick the movie.

On screen, the blonde who was eating her body weight in chocolate chucks the whole box at the TV. *Hm.* The idea has merit. I eye the takeout container in my hand.

"Don't do it," Guy tells me.

I blow out a breath and try to focus on the movie and not on the emptiness in my chest.

"Every storm runs out of rain," Guy says.

I blink at him. "What?"

"Scarlett's Granny told me that once, and it's true. Piper loves you. It will work out."

"How do you know?"

He shrugs. "It always does."

"What if she never forgives me? I don't know how to go on without her."

"Maybe you should try to learn how to go on with you. You're a good person, Oliver, even if you don't always believe it. You'll get through this. We're your friends. We'll be here for you no matter what. Don't give up hope."

Carson sniffs. "That was so beautiful."

Hope. Another thing that reminds me of Piper.

Her words float back to me, from what was basically our first date even if neither of us realized it at the time: "Hope is what keeps you from giving up. It's being bruised and battered and torn and going on anyway."

I can choose hope because I choose Piper. I'm not going to lose her. I'm going to prove that she can trust me with her heart and that we're both worthy of love.

It's a terrifying thought, but I know Piper. She's scared too. We can be scared together.

"How do we feel about Julia Roberts's movies?" Carson asks.

I lean back in the chair, shutting my eyes. *Well, things can't possibly get any worse.*

PIPER

My blaring cell phone jerks me awake. I haven't been sleeping. I've been miserable, wondering if I'm too broken to trust anyone ever again. Wondering if I made a mistake. Knowing I've made a mistake.

I want Oliver. I understand why he did what he did, even though I wish he'd told me. He was protecting me. I overreacted. Ben showing up at my door threw me off kilter. My emotions were raw, my mind a tunnel of distress, and I took it out on Oliver.

Mindy and I reported Ben's vague threats to the police, adding it to the report about the packages and texts. They didn't seem to care very much, but at least I have his activities on record if he tries anything else. There's a trail now.

On the bright side, work is going great. My *Hope* piece is

coming together quicker than I would have thought possible. But my heart is smashed to shit.

I fumble for my phone and put it to my ear blindly. "Hello?"

"Piper? Wake up. You need to look online."

I push my blankets down. "Taylor? What's going on?"

"Google yourself and then call me back as soon as you can." She hangs up.

Google myself? Confused, I pull up the web browser on my phone, blinking in confusion at the screen and the news results that pop up after I type in my own name.

Blake Bonham Cheating Scandal.

I gasp, sitting up. *What? Did the press find out about Mindy and Blake? How?*

I scroll down the results screen.

Blake Bonham Cheats with Reclusive Artist.

Wait. Artist? It can't be... me?

I click one of the links. There's a picture. Blake and I stand on the front stoop of the apartment, holding coffee and a bag of breakfast, our faces close together, both of us smiling.

Oh God. It was when he dropped the bag, and I picked it up, and we had that horrid moment. Yeah, we're both smiling and laughing. Awkwardly. The shot captured the moment we moved away from each other, so it looks like we were canoodling.

I groan and keep skimming through articles. It gets worse. *Blake Bonham Love Triangle with Oliver Nichols.*

Oh shit.

There are photos of me and Oliver too. From his birthday—sitting in the grass, drinking champagne and eating cupcakes. From our food truck lunch—his hand on my back as I climb into his car.

I wince and wonder what Oliver is going to think when he sees this. *What if he thinks I engineered all this to get back at him or something?* He doesn't trust people. He's notoriously private. Regina Charles she blabbed to the press, and he broke up with her to avoid exactly this.

Part of me thought Oliver and I would work out, but now... this might ruin any hope.

I scroll down and skim the comments on one of the articles:

Who is this Piper Fox, and why would men like Blake Bonham pant after her? She isn't even that hot.

I guess she's an artist, but I checked out her stuff, and it sucks balls.

Piper Fox? Not really a fox. She looks like a ferret with a bad haircut.

So she's a homewrecker and a slut. Got it.

My stomach churning with humiliation and disbelief, I back out of the article. I've had my fair share of criticism in the art world, but getting caught up in it is pointless and depressing. I continue glancing over headlines, and my stomach drops, my heart pounding frantically, when I reach the next link.

"There's a video?"

Thoughts tumble around in my mind. *Video of who? I*

know it can't be a video of me with Blake Bonham. What if it's me and Oliver?

Oh shit. Ben said he had something. How would he get something like that?

Nausea churns in my belly. I have to know. I have to watch it.

I take a few deep breaths and click one of the links. The recording is fuzzy with darkness, but Mindy's white couch is easy to make out. *Okay. Okay.* I relax a little. It can't be me and Ben. Or me and Oliver. Neither has ever been in Mindy's apartment, and Ben was only in the doorway.

The angle is from the bookshelf next to the TV. A sinking realization floods my chest. The statue. The Greatest Dad Award. That's where the video is shooting from. Ben put a camera in it. There's no other explanation.

Two figures appear on the screen, accompanied by the low murmur of voices and laughter. The couple kisses, hugging, then they tumble onto the couch together, Blake on the bottom. His features are discernible, despite the low lighting, but the woman has her back to the camera. Her hair is shorter than mine.

Oh no. I strain my eyes, focusing intently when her face turns slightly, exposing a partial angle, the hint of a cheek, the side of a nose. I drop the phone onto my duvet and cover my face my with hands.

It's Mindy. It's Blake and Mindy. *Shit.* But everyone in the world thinks it's me, except for the people directly involved.

I pick up the phone, kill the video, and then heave myself

out of bed, my heart pounding as I race into the living room and lift the statue. I want to smash it.

Wait. There has to be something illegal about all this. I can't smash it no matter how much I want to. It's evidence. But I can't let it stay here, watching and listening to us, either.

Grimacing, I go into the kitchen and place the statue it in one of the drawers. Not good enough. I march back to the living room, grab a couple of throw pillows from the couch ,and thrust them on top of the statue.

Now the drawer won't shut. The pillows are too big. I push at them, working the drawer closed and shoving in the fabric that keeps popping back out.

"You told me you were separated." Mindy's voice seeps through the thin wall.

I stop wrestling with the pillows and freeze.

"That's not the point." Blake's lower baritone is just as audible. "The point is how it looks—you know that."

I can't listen in to their private conversation if I can help it. I race back to my room and shut the door, taking a deep breath and leaning back against it. Everything is quiet.

Until they move into the living room. "You lied to me," Mindy says.

Silence. Footsteps.

"Don't leave like this." Her voice cracks. "Please."

I rub my head. I've never heard Mindy sound so desolate. Or so desperate.

"I have to go. You, of all people, should understand."

The front door shuts. I wait a minute before leaving my

room. Mindy is standing in the kitchen in her robe, her arms wrapped around herself, staring at the pillow-stuffed drawer I couldn't manage to shut.

"Mindy?" I say softly.

She faces me. She's not crying. Her face is empty and wrung out. "You've seen it?"

"I didn't watch it. Not past the first few seconds. I thought it might be something Ben took of us and then manipulated." I wince. I almost wish that were the case. Anything is better than the dead space in Mindy's eyes.

"I'm so sorry, Piper. The things they're saying about you because of something I did."

"It's okay." I step forward and put my arm over her shoulders. "It's not you who did this—it's Ben. And honestly, I don't know what to feel right now." Other than sick to my stomach with guilt because this is more my fault than hers.

If only I had never met Ben. If only I had left him earlier... I shake the thoughts away. I can't change the past. "I'm worried about you too. What did Blake say?"

Her hand slashes through the air in a dismissive motion. "It doesn't matter. It's over. He can't leave her now."

"What? Why not?"

"I can't think about him right at the moment." She steps out of my partial embrace. Her eyes fall shut, and she takes a deep breath and lets it out, her shoulders straightening on the exhalation. She opens her eyes, resolute. "Don't worry. I'm going fix this. I'm going to fix all of it. I'll make sure your reputation comes out of this unscathed. It won't impact your career."

I shake my head slowly. "I'm not worried about me. I'm worried about you."

Her phone vibrates. "I have to take this. I know I don't have to tell you, but don't talk to anyone until I can come up with a plan. And stay inside. There are probably paparazzi loitering outside, just waiting for you to leave."

I nod, knowing she needs to feel in control of something. "I have to call Taylor back," I say.

It speaks to how messed up Mindy is that she answers her phone without further comment, moving into the living room to pace.

"Ally, hey. Call the firm's attorneys. I know who obtained this video—it was done illegally. There will likely be criminal and civil charges, so the authorities should be involved as well. Work on getting our team in touch with every media outlet and get the videos shut down. Call Austin and work with him and Blake's PR guy on mitigating the rumors and deciding how we're going to spin this. Blake's lawyer might get involved too. Hell, maybe even Oliver Nichols, although that story was the only part that held any truth."

From her voice, you would never know Mindy looks like she got hit by a truck.

My mind is in overdrive. Now what? She can't be considering telling the truth just to protect me. That would be career suicide, and Mindy's whole life has been her work.

I escape back to my room to call Taylor, but before I can,

my phone dings with an incoming text. My stomach flip flops. *What if it's Ben, gloating?* I glance at the screen, and relief flows through me, followed immediately by a wave of anxiety.

It's from Oliver—only two words: *What happened?*

I scrub a hand over my face. At least he's not accusing me of anything.

I blow out a breath and then type: *Ben. He put a camera in the statuette he sent with those other crap sculptures. He must have been following us.*

A second after I hit Send, he responds: *If you need anything, I'm here.*

I sink down onto my bed, staring at the words, overwhelmed. He's not mad. He's not accusing me of anything. He's offering assistance. Offering his care yet again. And I know with bone-deep certainty that if I call him right now, he'll drop everything and do anything I ask, even if it means burning down the world.

I should never have doubted him. I was so scared I would lose myself in someone again. Things were moving so fast. Things with Ben moved fast too. I was terrified I would give too much, lose my sense of self again, but with Oliver, that was never a risk.

Ben was all about taking. Oliver is all about giving. He gave me everything I asked for, even when it was time away from him to settle my fears. I can't be afraid anymore.

Thirty~Two

O LIVER

"Incoming," Carson calls right as my inbox chimes with a message.

It's a press release. Blake Bonham and Rebel Records both released statements. Blake publicly admitted to *crossing a line* and stated that it was not with Piper Fox but with a mutual acquaintance. His comment also included the obligatory, *I am deeply sorry for my irresponsible and selfish behavior. Jeanette and I are committed to moving forward and ask for kindness and sensitivity for our privacy during this trying time.*

The Rebel Records statement is more circumspect, detailing only an ongoing investigation of the allegations, including criminal charges and civil suits being slung at one Ben Simon for stalking, nonconsensual pornography, libel, and defamation among other things.

I'll have to see if I can get in on some of that legal action. I rub my hands together. "Has he been arrested yet?" I call.

Carson materializes in the doorway. "No. According to the NYPD and every media source I have, Ben's in the wind. No one can find him. Cops are trying to issue a warrant. They're being pressured by Rebel Records' lawyers."

I nod. "Make sure we add our own pressure."

"Already on it."

It nearly kills me not to call or text Piper again, but I must respect her wishes.

The next night, I get a text: *Will you meet me in my studio at 11 tomorrow morning?*

As if she even has to ask. As if I could offer her anything other than an affirmation.

Yes, I reply.

At ten thirty, I'm pacing in my office. I can't think straight. I couldn't eat breakfast. My stomach is in knots. I haven't slept in a week. I haven't shaved in three days.

"Don't go down there yet," Carson calls from his desk.

"Don't tell me what to do."

"You have to play it somewhat cool."

I pass him, heading for the elevator. "I don't have to play it anything."

He sighs.

The elevator ride downstairs lasts fourteen years. By the time I get to the door of her studio, it's 10:33. I can't possibly wait until eleven. I key in the code and open the door.

She's working on a tall structure. Her back is to me. She's

crouched down, mask on, torch in hand, welding something along the bottom of the figure.

The piece is only partially finished, and I'm already awestruck. I can envision what it will be because it's exactly what she described when she passionately defended the topic on our first date. Hope.

The disjointed figure is distinctly feminine. The face and arms are scarred and bedraggled. Ropes and chains attempt to drag her down, the bottom part of the structure filled with jagged pieces, yet she's rising. Fighting. Persisting against all odds.

Some of the metal pieces are familiar, though they have been melted and fused to form the body. They are from the box we brought back from Whitby.

The first time I saw Piper, she was emotionally wrecked and exhausted, a frail shadow of the woman before me. Even then, I recognized her inner core of strength. She's a fighter. She's incredible.

The torch dies. She stands, pushing the welding mask up on her head. "Oliver." She licks her lips. "You're early."

"Hi." *Brilliant. Hi. That's the best I could come up with?*

The corner of her mouth kicks up, but then her gaze flickers to something over my shoulder, and she freezes. Panic fills her eyes. Her mouth opens, but no sound emerges.

My heart pumps, the throbbing almost loud enough to override the scuffle of footsteps behind me.

Something hard and cold presses into the back of my neck. "You think you can have everything that's rightfully mine, but look at you now. I'm the one who can take it all away." The voice is low and trembling with bitterness. The gun jabs harder into my neck.

I focus on Piper. Her eyes are wide with horror, fixed on the man standing behind me. My mind fractures. One part of me is fully present, inside this situation, recognizing that Piper's expression, twisting in terror, might be the last thing I see.

Another part of me—the part that has already lived through hell and faced the prospect of death and then come out on the other side—is seething and ready to do anything it takes to remove the threat in the environment. He won't hurt her. I won't allow it.

How the hell did he get in here? How dare he come into my residence and put Piper through this.

"What do you want?" I keep my voice light and easy, but my muscles are locking, my mind turning over options and alternatives.

The gun digs harder into my neck. "You ruined everything. You took her from me. Like you don't already have enough."

I grit my teeth. As if Piper were a *thing* someone could take.

"He's not the one you're mad at. I'm the one who left." Piper's voice quavers, her hand flexing around the torch still in her hand.

"You," Ben spits. "You've been ignoring me. Like I mean nothing." He moves the gun from my skin. "I mean something now, don't I?"

The barrel moves into my peripheral vision, pointing at Piper.

No. Every cell in my body revolts. I twist and reach in one sharp movement and yank the weapon down. Adrenaline pounds through me, sharpening details—the black matte of the gun, the dots on the grip, the smell of Ben's cologne mixed with the acridness of sweat and booze. His brown shirt.

Brown shirt. The delivery guy. That's how he got in.

We struggle over the firearm, my fingers slipping off the barrel. Time spreads and slows, our grappling tug-of-war interminable, like the drip of sap down a tree.

The gun fires. My ears go numb and the world goes muted except a faint ringing. Time resumes at a frantic pace.

A tall figure emerges from the direction of the garage, jumps on top of Ben, and tumbles all of us to the floor. My elbow slams into the concrete. Brienne is sprawling on top of Ben, holding his arms down while he gasps for air after falling straight on his back.

The gun. Where is it? I have to get the gun. My eyes alight on an inch of the black grip pinned under Ben's shoulder.

I yank it out from underneath him and fling it to the side, out of reach. My ears are still ringing. Distantly, I wonder if I'm in shock. Nothing seems real.

Trembling hands pat my shoulders and down the front of my body. My eyes find Piper crouching in front of me. Her mouth moves, but no sound emerges over the buzzing reverberation in my ears. Her head is cocked at an angle to keep her phone in place between her cheek and shoulder.

She jerks on my suit jacket. Dazed, I help her tug it off. I glance down. A blood stain spreads along the left sleeve of my shirt. It's a lot of blood.

"I'm bleeding."

She presses on the wound, and a sharp sting breaks through the numb shell surrounding me, burning fire spreading on my arm. Grimacing, I try to ignore the pain and focus on Piper. Her eyes are on my arm, and she presses her hand against the wound. Her expression is tight, her mouth still moving as she speaks with whomever is on the phone—the authorities, most likely, I decide in a detached way.

Her hair is tousled around her face, and I reach to push back the strands but use my injured arm.

She scowls at me. "Stay still." The words are faint but legible through the ringing in my head.

I smile, and for some reason her eyes fill with tears. My smile falters. I don't want her to cry.

People fill the room, and activity blurs around me, like it's all happening to someone else and I'm merely an observer. Time becomes as wispy as smoke.

The paramedics arrive, my arm is wrapped, and I'm carted into an ambulance filled with IV fluids and taken to a nearby medical center. Panic threatens the corners of my mind. The only thing keeping me sane is Piper's hand in mine. She stays with me, tethering me to reality.

At the hospital, I'm cleaned and stitched and given pain medication and I don't even know what else, but I think I fall asleep.

When I return to consciousness, I'm lying in a hospital

bed. The lights are dim, with sunlight trying to break in around the edges of the curtained window. Everything is white—walls, sheets, floor.

Piper is tucked into a chair near my bed, her eyes closed. I shift, trying to sit up.

"You're awake." She rubs her eyes before moving closer then twining her fingers with mine while one hand fusses, straightening my blanket. "Are you comfortable? Do you need anything? Water?"

I nod, and she hands me a disposable cup without releasing my hand.

I chug the liquid down. "When can I leave?"

"Soon." She swallows, her fingers tightening. "You were grazed by a bullet. You needed stitches, but they were more worried about the shock. Are you feeling okay?"

I nod. Although my mind is a little fuzzy, it's nothing compared to the moments after Ben... "What happened? Is everyone okay?"

"Everyone is fine. You had the worst injury." The corner of her mouth tips down, her brow puckering as she searches my eyes. "Ben's been arrested. They added assault with a deadly weapon to his litany of charges. The cops were here earlier, and I gave them a statement. So did Brienne. She's been texting me updates, but you haven't missed much other than that. You'll have to talk to the cops eventually."

I nod.

Her smile is tremulous. She shifts closer to me, blinking rapidly. "I was so worried about you." Her voice wavers.

"Hey. I'm okay. Come here." I maneuver to one side, tugging on her fingers to pull her closer.

Without hesitation, she scrambles in next to me on the narrow bed and rests her face in the crook of my good arm, the tip of her nose cold against the skin of my neck. She takes a deep breath and relaxes, sinking farther into me.

For the first time in days, a tightness inside me releases and settles, and I can breathe again.

"Are you in pain?" she asks.

"No."

She lifts her head from my shoulder, her hand sliding along my bristled cheek. "You haven't shaved."

"I didn't want to."

She searches my face. "You haven't been sleeping well."

Her words... a smile tugs at my lips. Every word I've exchanged with Piper Fox is seared into my very being. I know what comes next. "Have you?"

She bites her lip. "Touché."

Hope surges to life, bursting through me. I move the conversation ahead to my favorite part. "I want you."

Her smile is the sun breaking through the clouds and warming all my cold, dark corners.

"I mean, I need you," I continue. But then I have to deviate from the original script. "And I absolutely mean all of it."

Her arms lift around my neck, her leg sliding over my waist. She molds her body against me, and then her lips slide against mine.

"I'm so sorry." She continues to kiss me, murmuring

against my lips, her fingers rubbing my jaw, her words falling out in between the pleasurable assault. "I wanted you to meet me this morning so I could tell you. I'm sorry I didn't trust you. I'm sorry I didn't call you sooner. I'm sorry I didn't tell you about everything. I missed you so much. I thought I was going to lose you today." Her voice cracks.

Bliss is buoyant heat fizzing in my chest and expanding to my limbs. We kiss and touch and whisper sweet words, relearning the scent of each other. We hold each other for an eternity. It's not long enough. My one hand is in her hair, making the messy tendrils even messier, and the other hand —my injured arm—finds the best resting place possible and cups her bottom. Perfection.

Or not. She pulls away from me. Her eyes are troubled.

"What's wrong?"

"I'm not going to have all the pieces done in time for the exhibit."

"I know."

Her brows lift. "You do?"

"You aren't exactly an accomplished liar. I suspected something was amiss when you first came to me with your space issue, and then my suspicions deepened when Finley asked you how your work was going at dinner, and you said it was great the same way someone describes a recent root canal."

She winces. "I guess I'm more transparent than I thought."

"It's fine. I have a plan."

Her head cocks. "What's your plan?"

"We'll feature *Hope* at the opening. Then we'll announce that a new piece of yours will be highlighted each month."

"Each month?"

I shrug. "Or longer. Two months, three months. If it takes longer, it takes longer. That way, we can get people intrigued and keep them coming back."

Her eyes search mine. "You would do that for me?"

I scoff. "I'm doing it for me. The marketing potential is limitless."

She grins, ducking her head back down against my chest.

I rub her scalp with my fingers, brushing a kiss over the top of her head. "In exchange, all I ask is that you let me help Mindy annihilate Ben in court after the criminal charges are exhausted."

She lifts her head again, resting her chin on my chest. "Have at it. I wouldn't deprive you of the pleasure."

My mind goes darkly thoughtful, imagining all the ways I—or, well, my lawyers—can make him pay.

"I have my own revenge planned," she adds.

I push aside thoughts of legal vengeance to focus on her face. "What's that?"

Her smile could only be described as mischievous. "I'm going to be happy."

I lift my brows. "How will you accomplish such a thing?"

She pushes herself up a little, infusing her voice with gravity. "First, I need a man."

"Really." Humor pushes at me, but I keep my tone dry.

She tilts her head as if considering all her options. "Preferably a billionaire."

"Well. There can't be many of those just lying around."

She presses her lips together. "He also has to be a ruthless businessman with a soft and gooey center."

"Hm. That seems to be a growing trait for billionaires."

"And the dealbreaker is..." She moves closer, her nose brushing mine. "He has to be excellent at cross-stitch."

I bark out a laugh. "You'll never find such a paragon. A true unicorn."

"Oh, he is." She's all smug glee.

When our amusement subsides, her eyes go dark and serious.

"What is it?" I ask.

"I love you," she whispers.

Astonishment rushes through me.

She covers my lips with her fingers. "You don't have to say it back. I know it's a new concept for you." Her smile is wry. "But I want you to know how I feel."

Emotion clogs my throat. I don't know how to express what she is to me. She's where I belong, where I fit.

I brush a strand of hair back behind her ear and cup her cheek in my palm. "You are everything I never knew I could hope for."

Her face fills with light. "I know."

PIPER

"Come on. It's about to start." I tug on Oliver's hand, glancing over my shoulder at him as we edge around food and craft stalls on the outskirts of the Whitby town green.

Our eyes lock for a second, and he smiles. He looks delectable in a fitted sage green T-shirt and jeans, his face lined with scruff. The small grin he tosses me catapults him from attractive to downright gorgeous.

A frisson of exhilaration shoots through me. He's mine. All mine.

Hundreds of people are spread out on the lawn as if everyone in a twenty-mile radius has come out to witness Whitby's annual Independence Day Extravaganza. During the day, there are booths for local businesses, a concert in the park, and other activities, and at dusk, the best fireworks display around.

"How are we going to find them?" Oliver asks as we weave through families on blankets and camp chairs, side-stepping to avoid colliding with a child who runs by, waving a sparkler.

"We always set up in the same spot. At least, we used to." It's been years since I've been here for the Fourth of July.

We would have been here earlier, but I was distracted by work. I hit my stride and was completely in the zone, finishing up work on *Hope*, and Oliver didn't want to disturb me until it was imperative that we hit the road. Not to mention, once he did interrupt me, we got sidetracked on the couch in my studio. It wasn't the first time we christened the space, and it probably won't be the last. After all, we have to remove any lingering bad vibes over and over and over again.

A high-pitched whine cuts through the air, and an explosion of white light bursts overhead, crackling outward in a shower of sparks. Oliver stops, his hand still in mine, halting my forward progression. I face him.

His head is tilted upward, his eyes gleaming in the darkness. "I haven't seen fireworks since I was a kid." Another firework explodes. As the light fades overhead, he squeezes my hand. "Let's hurry."

Stopping periodically to gaze up at the show, we jog and weave through the throng until we reach the north end of the gazebo in the center of the town green. The arguing reaches my ears before we reach their blankets.

"A hot dog is not a sandwich." Jake reclines on an old pink quilt, propped up on his hands, his head pointed toward Archer.

Archer and Finley are lying together on a darker blanket next to him, while Taylor sits on the quilt by Jake, cross-legged and eating popcorn.

"It's meat between two slices of bread," Archer says. "It's the definition of a sandwich."

A flurry of fireworks bursts and crackles above us.

"Peanut butter doesn't have meat, but it still makes a sandwich," Jake argues.

Taylor chucks a piece of popcorn at Jake. "Shut up and watch the show."

"What does peanut butter have to do with anything?" Archer chuckles.

Just then, Finley spots our approach and waves us over. "You made it just in time! Come, sit."

We squeeze on the blankets with everyone, with greetings and hugs all around. We end up somewhere in the middle of the group. I have Finley on one side and Oliver on the other.

I lean into him, the heat of his arm curving around my back and notching us together like puzzle pieces, and we gaze up at the colorful explosions filling the night sky.

Archer lifts his head over Finley and me to look at Oliver. "Do you think a hot dog is a sandwich?"

Oliver frowns. "I suppose it meets the technical definition of a sandwich."

"Ha!" Jake raises a fist.

"However," Oliver continues, "it's not acceptable vernacular to refer to a hot dog as a sandwich or a sandwich as a hot dog."

"Ha ha!" Archer calls to Jake.

"This is bullshit," Jake says.

Their argument continues, and Finley edges a little closer to me. "Mindy couldn't make it?" she murmurs.

"She's meeting with Blake tomorrow morning," I whisper back, keeping my focus on the sky.

Taylor crawls over and stops in front of us. "What are we talking about? Is it Mindy? She still avoiding me?"

I wave a hand. "No. It's not you. She has other things going on."

"Things involving a certain soulful-eyed singer?" Taylor presses.

I spread my hands. "She hasn't been sharing much."

Taylor snorts. "You don't think it's ironic that Miss I'm So Perfect, who never does anything even slightly wrong, did something, like, majorly wrong?"

"Taylor." Finley gives her the mom voice.

Taylor exhales a disgruntled sigh and leans back on the blanket, turning her stony face skyward.

Even if I knew more of what was happening, I wouldn't share Mindy's private struggles with Taylor—not with the way their relationship has been going. Mindy only gave me the basics, anyway. She's been on edge because of work, and it didn't help that Blake went radio silent. Mindy has been put on administrative leave while Rebel Records investigates her connection to the whole scandal. I'm not sure who leaked the truth—whether Mindy slipped pieces of it to her assistant or someone else at work or if Blake said something or if someone just figured it out from watching the video. But they're looking into the ramifications of her being even loosely involved with a client and the resulting media attention.

Fortunately, after Ben was arrested—and many lawsuits were flung around—most media outlets retracted the story about the love triangle between Blake and Oliver and me and pulled down the videos. It didn't entirely stop the nonsense—the internet holds onto things forever—but the furor has died down.

After the fireworks end, we stay on the blankets and talk, waiting for the crowd to thin. Taylor is staying the night but leaving tomorrow—she never remains in one place for long. Archer and Jake and Oliver continue the sandwich-and-hot-dog debate, but eventually, we pack up the blankets and snacks and head to the parking lot.

"We'll meet you back at home," I say to Finley when we have to split to get to our respective vehicles.

"Meet us at the main house so we can hang out for a bit?" Finley says.

I nod.

"We cleaned up the cabin Oliver stayed in last month for you both to sleep in." She grins and waves as they turn away.

We wait in a line of cars attempting to exit the park. We aren't in a hurry.

Oliver leans back in the driver's seat and looks at me. "Thank you for inviting me this weekend."

I reach for him, and our fingers tangle together. "Of course," I say, surprised by his gratitude. I thought it was assumed we would spend the holiday together. "You're always invited. I'm not sure I can sleep without you, actually. I'm addicted now."

He chuckles, his hand squeezing mine.

We haven't spent a night apart since the whole Ben debacle. Mostly, we stay at his place, but some nights, he comes over to Mindy's. I haven't wanted to leave her on her own too much. I think we annoy her a little with our constant touches and heated looks, but I can't control it. I don't think he can either.

"Will you come with me to Guy and Scarlett's wedding? Since I'm a groomsman, I may be busy for parts of it, but... I want you to be there."

My brows lift, my mouth stretching with a smile. "I would love to go with you."

We roll forward a few more feet, and when we come to a complete stop, he stretches over the center console, his lips grazing mine. "You make me believe in love." His words are a heated brush against my skin. "You make me feel like—" He swallows "Like I might actually be worthy of it."

My heart swells, a twisting expansion pressing on my rib cage, the emotion filling me, too overwhelming to be contained by the small organ. I reach up, cupping his face in my palms, and then I kiss him. The kiss deepens immediately, both of us eager and desperate within seconds, unable to get close enough with the console acting as an inconvenient barrier between our bodies. His lips are warm and firm, and he tastes like beauty and devotion, like summer nights and falling in love.

A car horn blares, breaking us apart. I laugh, shaky with lingering exhilaration. He doesn't let go of me or make any moves to resume our drive, unconcerned with the impatient driver behind us.

His thumb brushes my cheek, and his serious eyes lock on mine. "I love you." His voice is low and assured.

"I love you so much." Emotion builds inside me, spilling out of my eyes.

His mouth sweeps my skin, my lips, my eyes, my cheeks, his touch stroking away my tears. "I love you," he says over and over between kisses, as if the words tumble out and he can't stop them.

Happiness is a glow in my chest that can't be contained, not even when more cars honk around us. The sounds fade into the background, and all that's left is me and Olive and the whispered words of love between us.

The End

———

Next in the Fox Family Series is Mindy and Luke's story: Another Fox Bites the Dust, coming Spring/Summer 2023!

• • •

If you didn't get a chance to check out Finley and Archer's book, *Between a Fox and a Hard Place,* it's available now everywhere books are sold!

Also by Mary Frame

Imperfect Series:

Book One: Imperfect Chemistry

Book Two: Imperfectly Criminal

Book Three: Practically Imperfect

Book Four: Picture Imperfect

Book Five: Imperfect Strangers

Book Six: Imperfectly Delicious

The Dorky Duet (Plus a companion novel!)

Ridorkulous

Geektastic

Nerdelicious

Time after Time Series:

Time of My Life

If I Could Turn Back Time

Castle Cove Mystery Series

Fake It to the Limit

Too Much Crime on My Hands

You're the Con That I Want

Brand New Small Town Rom Coms

The Fox Family Series:

Between a Fox and a Hard Place

The Fox and the Rebound

Another Fox Bites the Dust